"I think we can benefit each other."

Murad's tone was casual, but his words caused a surge of excitement in Eleanore.

"Did I miss something?" she asked.

"Well, I'm having a little trouble relating to my employees," he admitted. "So I thought that if you were to act as my hostess at various social functions . . ."

Eleanore sighed. What if he had ulterior motives for moving her into his house? But her common sense quickly squashed that idea. Murad most assuredly wasn't starving for attention. Making up her mind, she said, "I accept."

"Good." His brief smile made him boyishly appealing. "I'll send a car for you."

"I'll be waiting," she said hesitantly, still wondering if he had seduction on his mind. It suddenly occurred to her that she'd be devastated if he didn't. . . .

Judith McWilliams had no choice but to write *The Royal Treatment*. The princely Arab Murad Ahiquar was originally a minor character in Judith's fifth Temptation, *Honorable Intentions*. Feedback from readers was so enthusiastic that Judith realized Murad's story had to be told. *The Royal Treatment* has all the warmth and humor Judith is known for... and a fairy-tale ending!

Judith, her husband and their four children now make their home in Indiana.

Books by Judith McWilliams

HARLEQUIN TEMPTATION
78—POLISHED WITH LOVE
103—IN GOOD FAITH
119—SERENDIPITY
160—NO RESERVATIONS
184—HONORABLE INTENTIONS

The Royal Treatment
JUDITH MCWILLIAMS

Harlequin Books

TORONTO • NEW YORK • LONDON
AMSTERDAM • PARIS • SYDNEY • HAMBURG
STOCKHOLM • ATHENS • TOKYO • MILAN

Published June 1989

ISBN 0-373-25353-2

1

"IT'S NOT THE END of the world. It's not the end of the world." Eleanore Fulton chanted aloud as she crossed the lobby of her apartment building. Reaching the elevator, she inserted her key in the lock box, pushed the up button and then sagged against the wall, waiting for the elevator to arrive.

"Eleanore? Eleanore!" An impatient voice cut into her chaotic thoughts. "I've been trying to get your attention ever since you came in. Are you sick?"

"Unto the very depths of my soul." Eleanore's dark brown eyes lit with reluctant humor.

"Quoting Shakespeare at people at ten o'clock in the morning is not the way to win friends and influence people. And speaking of the time, why aren't you at school, teaching? Did I forget a holiday or something?"

"If it is, it's a black one." Eleanore grimaced. "I was, to put it delicately, let go this morning."

"Let go?" Liz stared blankly at her. "Let go where?"

"Out the door." Eleanore shrugged her slender shoulders. "Out into the great big world of the unemployed." She stepped into the elevator as its doors opened with a reluctant groan.

"The school board couldn't have fired you!" Liz sputtered indignantly as she followed her into the elevator. "Why, they even gave you a plaque last year for being an outstanding teacher of the learning disabled."

"I wonder if I could pawn it?"

"Eleanore," Liz wailed, "be serious."

"If I get any more serious, I'm going to start crying." Eleanore automatically tucked a wayward strand of dark brown hair into the chignon at her nape.

"You aren't the type. Besides, they can't fire you. You have tenure."

"Had—past tense. And I wasn't fired. I was laid off."

"But why? Did you make someone mad?"

"Oh, no. The superintendent didn't want to do it any more than I wanted it done to me. It all boils down to a question of money. Or more accurately, a lack of it."

"But New York City's educational budget is enormous."

"So's the number of students they service," Eleanore pointed out. "Unfortunately, most of the money for the learning disabled comes from state and federal funds. And the amount of the funding is directly tied to how many L.D. kids we have in the system." She paused as the elevator stopped on the eleventh floor.

"I'm coming with you." Liz followed her into the hallway. "I want to hear the rest of it and, besides, you shouldn't be alone."

"And you shouldn't believe everything you read in those psychology books of yours," Eleanore said tartly. "I have no intention of going off the deep end and, anyway, I won't be alone. You're forgetting that Kelly is here."

"I wish I could forget that cousin of yours. She's nothing but a leech, financially and emotionally."

"In the first place, having been raised with her, I consider Kelly more of a sister than a cousin. And in the second—"

"I know. It's none of my business." Liz grimaced apologetically. "It's just that you're my friend, and it infuriates me to see the way Kelly's taken over your life. Ever since she decided to wallow in unwed motherhood and let you foot the bill, you haven't even been out on a date."

"It hasn't been that bad."

"It's been worse," Liz insisted. "And you're not getting any younger."

"Very few of us do." Eleanore grinned at her indignant friend.

Liz frowned. "Will you be serious. We're both going to be thirty this winter."

"Well, I won't tell anyone if you won't." Eleanore inserted her key in the tarnished lock of her door.

"But—"

"Drop it." She gave Liz a level look. "Your fears to the contrary, I am not being taken advantage of. I knew exactly what I was getting into when I told Kelly she could move in with me last year. Besides, this arrangement isn't going to last forever. Kelly will be starting classes next week at City College. In a few years, she'll be able to support both herself and the baby."

"If you say so," Liz muttered, her doubts clearly written on her face.

"I do." Eleanore pushed open the door. "Would you like a cup of coffee?"

"No, all I want is information. How could the school administration get rid of someone with tenure?" Liz glanced around the empty living room. "I thought you said Kelly was here."

"She probably took Lacey to the park. It's a gorgeous day for it."

Kicking off her shoes, Eleanore sank down onto the sofa, leaned back and closed her eyes.

"You look like you could use a good stiff drink," Liz said bluntly. "You're the color of skim milk."

"Thanks, that's just what I needed. A kind word."

"And what I need is an informative one. You still haven't told me how they can get rid of a teacher with tenure."

"Easy, if there aren't sufficient students to fill a class, even a tenured teacher can be given her walking papers."

"But why you in particular? You're good. Damned good."

"Because I have the least seniority of the tenured teachers in the L.D. program. There was nothing personal in my going. In fact, my principal has spent the last three days calling everyone he could think of trying to get funding for my salary, but he couldn't. Money is incredibly tight in education this year."

"It's going to be tight around here too without you bringing in a salary." Liz said, going straight to the heart of the matter. "I don't have much saved, but what there is, you're welcome to borrow."

"Thanks, Liz. I appreciate the thought, but I've got enough in the bank to pay the bills for a few months and my principal said he'd put my name at the top of the list for substitute teaching." She tried to sound enthusiastic.

"Substitute teaching!" Liz repeated in horror. "You can't be serious. You'd have a different class every day. A different group of little devils intent on making your life hell. Why don't you simply run numbers for the mob? It'd probably be safer."

"It won't be that bad. Besides, look on the bright side. I won't be in any one class long enough to be bored."

"No, simply long enough to be traumatized! Couldn't you try to find another teaching job?"

"Teaching jobs are scarcer than hen's teeth. And the few openings there were are filled, now that the school year's started."

"Kelly should get a job and help out."

"She is helping . . . by learning a skill for the future. Substitute teaching may not be great, but I can handle it as a stopgap. The principal's promised to get me back on the regular staff as soon as he can. I can manage," she insisted, as much to convince herself as Liz.

"Sure you'll manage, but at what cost?"

"Tell you what, if I crack under the strain, you can give me free psychological counseling."

"Ha! I've been telling you what to do for years and you haven't listened yet." Liz got to her feet. "Just you remember what I said about letting Kelly handle some of the responsibility. Why should you have to carry the whole burden?" With that, she left.

"Why indeed?" Eleanore muttered as she rubbed her aching forehead. Despite her denials to Liz, she was tired of the whole mess. Tired of being the one her family always leaned on. Tired of being the one who always had to figure out how they were going to solve a seemingly never-ending series of emotional and financial crises. It was a role she'd long ago been cast in by her loving but totally ineffectual aunt. A role Kelly seemed only too eager to perpetuate into the next generation.

Eleanore let out a long shuddering sigh. Just once, she would have liked to have let someone else do the worrying while she sat back, secure in the knowledge that everything was going to be just fine.

She shook her head at her unrealistic desire. There was no one to even help her, let alone shoulder the burden. Certainly not her heedless young cousin who flitted through life like a butterfly, sipping its pleasures with no thought for the consequences of her actions. Nor her vague, inept aunt and most assuredly not her alcoholic uncle.

If only she could have been raised in her own family instead of her Aunt Theresa's. If only her father hadn't deserted her mother when he'd found out that Eleanore was on the way. Then her poor mother wouldn't have found it necessary to give up her baby, and then— With the ease of long practice, Eleanore cut off her wayward thoughts. Dwelling on might-have-beens was not only morbid, but it was totally counterproductive. Wishing couldn't change reality. And the reality was that she no longer had a job.

The shrill buzzing of the doorbell interrupted her thoughts and gratefully she went to answer it. Right now, she welcomed any distraction, even one of the door-to-door salesmen who were forever eluding the building's lax security system. But it was Mrs. Benton, Eleanore's next-door neighbor.

"I thought I heard you come in," she said the moment Eleanore opened the door. "I know I promised your cousin that I'd watch Lacey until you got home from school this afternoon, but, since you're back now, you can take her." She held out the sleeping infant.

Eleanore automatically accepted the baby, cradling the tiny body against her shoulder. "Where did Kelly go, Mrs. Benton?"

"I don't know. Maybe the note she left for you says." She handed Eleanore a slightly smudged, sealed envelope. "Have a nice day," she added as she left.

"I don't know about nice, but it's certainly turning out to be memorable." Eleanore deftly shouldered the door closed. She smiled gently as she glanced down at the sleeping baby. Lacey was such a darling.

Eleanore carried her into the bigger of the apartment's two bedrooms, the one Lacey and Kelly shared. She lowered the baby into her crib, being very careful not to wake her.

Creeping softly from the bedroom, Eleanore closed the door behind her before slitting the envelope open and extracting the single handwritten sheet. Her heart sank as she read it.

"It only needed this," she muttered, staring at the scrawled words as if willing them to reform themselves into a more acceptable message. But to her dismay, they still spelled out the same appalling information. Kelly had left to "find" herself and asked Eleanore to take care of Lacey until she returned.

"Find herself!" Eleanore exploded. "I'll find her, and when I do I'll wring her fool neck!" How could Kelly blithely take off on a narcissistic voyage of self-discovery with no more thought for her daughter's welfare than a casual postscript to the note saying that her mother would probably baby-sit while Eleanore was teaching?

The fact that Kelly's mother lived on Long Island almost an hour's train trip away had been overlooked. As had the fact that she was not only crippled with arthritis, but had an alcoholic husband to cope with, as well. Eleanore crumpled the letter in frustration. Kelly had a positive genius for ignoring what she didn't want to face.

Eleanore pressed her forefinger against the bridge of her nose. Her nagging headache was fast escalating into a raging torrent of pain.

Sinking down on the couch, she forced herself to calmly count to ten before allowing herself to consider this latest development. It wasn't as bad as she'd first thought, she told herself grimly, it was worse.

Not only was her steady, if unspectacular, paycheck gone, but Kelly's desertion meant that she was going to have to pay out hefty sums to a child-care center so that Lacey would be cared for while she was substitute teaching.

Eleanore got to her feet and began to pace across the small living room, her thoughts going around in circles. If she had to pay a child-care center out of her meager earnings as a substitute, there wouldn't be enough left to pay all the bills. And that was assuming she would get work every day, which was by no means a certainty.

Eleanore took a deep breath and tried to stem her rising panic. There were her savings, she reminded herself. She had enough in the bank to pay the bills for a couple of months, even if she included the exorbitant cost of good day care. Surely she could find Kelly in that amount of time and make her understand that she had a responsibility to her daughter. A responsibility she couldn't simply dump in someone else's lap.

"MR. NICK CARLTON, Your Highness."

Bemused, Nick watched the door close behind the butler and then turned to his friend. "Where did you get him, Murad? Central casting?"

Murad's deep chuckle echoed through the luxurious study. "What brings you down to New York City, Nick?" He clasped his friend's hand with obvious pleasure. "I thought you were safely settled upstate with your new wife and son."

"Settled, but not safely. Jed has just discovered chemistry," Nick said darkly. "And that doesn't answer my question. What's going on around here? You never travel with more than a secretary and yet I spotted two maids, what looks like a gardener and that caricature of an English butler just between here and the front door."

"Caricature, nothing. Wilkerson is the genuine article. I stole him from my father's ambassador to London."

"Ah, petty larceny."

"You wouldn't say that if you knew what he cost me," Murad said ruefully. "So how's the fair Jenny?"

"Pregnant." Nick's face glowed with pride. "We came down to the city to outfit the nursery."

"Congratulations." Murad pounded him on the back. "May Allah grant you many sons."

"A daughter would be nice, too."

Murad sighed. "I can think of one daughter I could do without."

"You haven't been trifling with someone's affections, have you, Your Highness?" His eyes gleamed with mocking laughter.

"Knock it off, Nick."

"But you made such a show of using your title." Nick shoved the paper he was carrying at his friend. "You made quite a spectacle of yourself last night."

"Hmm." Murad studied the picture with evident satisfaction. "What do you think?"

"That you went to a great deal of trouble to promulgate the stereotype of a self-indulgent, free-spending, playboy Arab prince. The question is who are you trying to convince? And, more importantly, why? Murad, is there trouble back in Abar?"

"No, my father's throne is secure and my five older brothers are loving, if not particularly dutiful, sons. No, Nick, the trouble is right here in New York City. Specifically, in the offices that manage our family's investments in the U.S."

"Embezzlement?"

"Not precisely." Murad ran his long fingers through his gleaming black hair. "A few years ago, my father decided to concentrate the bulk of our American investments in real estate. Consequently, we've been buying up shopping malls, office buildings and land for development. What's been happening with increasing frequency is that word of our investment plans is being leaked and we're finding that crucial pieces of property we need to complete a project are being bought before we can get them and then sold back to us at exorbitant prices."

"By a dummy corporation, no doubt?"

"Exactly. I'm as sure as I can be that the individuals listed on the incorporation papers are fictitious. And to further complicate matters, the proceeds from the sales are being deposited directly into a numbered Swiss bank account.

"The leak has to be coming from someone in our New York office. Trying to find out which someone it is when I was still in Abar was impossible. So, since my father had intended me to take over the day-to-day management of our American investments next year anyway, he decided to send me now in the hope I can find the thief."

"And this ridiculous charade—" Nick gestured with the paper "—is to allay the fears of said thief?"

"Uh-huh. I want him to believe that I was only the titular head of Abar's Secret Service and that I'm no danger to anyone."

"If he believes that, you might have a go at selling him the Brooklyn Bridge." Nick laughed. "How about having dinner with us tonight? Jed's dying to meet the man who sent a gold statue encrusted with jewels as a wedding present. And he doesn't even know it was a fertility symbol."

"Don't knock it." Murad grinned. "It obviously worked."

Nick grinned back. "I'm going to have to have a little talk with you if you think that's what caused Jenny's pregnancy."

"*Inshallah,*" Murad murmured piously, his black eyes gleaming with laughter. "Unfortunately, I'll have to take a rain check on dinner tonight. I promised Selim I'd see his daughter as soon as possible."

"I thought Selim and Amineh never had any children, and that was why your father let you spend so much time with them when you were growing up."

"They didn't. Selim did."

"That's unexpected."

"To put it mildly." Murad grimaced. "I would have sworn I knew everything there was to know about the man and then I find out that thirty years ago, when he was a student at Columbia, he was seduced by an American woman."

"Seduced?" Nick asked in disbelief. "Selim's no fool."

"Not now," Murad agreed. "But thirty years ago he was a naive twenty-year-old who'd never even been out of Abar, while the woman in question was twenty-eight, a gorgeous blonde and twice divorced. Selim didn't stand a chance. To make a long story short, this Marilyn Fulton overestimated her hold on him. She knew he was promised to marry Amineh once he'd finished his education, but Marilyn thought if she got pregnant, he'd marry her instead. He didn't."

"Rough on the kid," Nick observed.

"Not financially. Selim told me he paid five thousand a month while the child was growing up, plus medical and education expenses."

"So why contact her after all this time?"

"Selim has always regretted not knowing his daughter, but he was afraid to see her for fear that Amineh would find out and be devastated by the knowledge that his mistress had been able to give him a child when she couldn't. Since Amineh died this past summer, she can no longer be hurt by the knowledge that Selim wants to bring his daughter home to Abar."

"But you're not talking about a child. You're talking about a thirty-year-old woman. You may not be doing Selim a favor by taking her back."

"I know. But Selim has aged ten years since Amineh's death. He needs something to interest him in living again, and if a long-lost daughter is what it takes, then that's what he'll get."

"I hope he doesn't get more than he bargained for. If what you say about the mother is true, the daughter might be as bad."

"I share your concern." Murad sighed. "But enough about my problems. Tell me how life as a farmer suits you."

"Yes, Aunt Theresa. Certainly. I'll tell Kelly. Lacey's fine. Still the cutest two-month-old I've ever seen." Eleanore made soothing sounds into the phone while frowning at her living-room wall. "I will. Take care of yourself, Aunt Theresa. I'll try to get out to see you sometime soon. Bye now."

Eleanore hung up in frustration. It was obvious that Kelly hadn't confided her plans to her mother and there was no way she could bring herself to tell Theresa of her daughter's abandonment of Lacey. It would serve no useful purpose and only give her aunt one more thing to worry about.

Picking up the sheet of paper she'd been studying before her aunt's phone call, Eleanore reread her notes. By calling every person she knew who had children, she'd been able to come up with the names of three places where she could leave Lacey while she worked.

Eleanore examined the short list. The day-care center was by far the most reliable choice, but their daily charges amounted to a little over half of what she would earn as a substitute teacher. There was no way she could survive on what would remain.

That left two private homes. Mrs. Patrick came highly recommended and her charges were affordable—just. The problem was, she only provided care on a weekly basis, which meant that even on those days when Eleanore didn't get called to substitute, Mrs. Patrick would still expect to be paid.

Eleanore frowned. Her principal had assured her that she'd be the first sub he called, and she believed him. But if no teacher was gone, then he couldn't call her. And with the school year just starting, it was possible that there wouldn't be many absences. Most teachers tried to save their sick days for the blustery winter months when it was so easy to catch a cold or the flu from their pupils.

She did some quick calculations. If she didn't get at least three days work a week, then Mrs. Patrick would cost as large a percentage of her income as the day-care center would.

Reluctantly, she dropped her gaze to the last name on the list, a Mrs. Burton. Her fees were about the same as Mrs. Patrick's, but she was willing to provide casual care, only charging when Eleanore actually used her services. Moreover, she lived in the apartment building. But there was something about her... Eleanore grimaced as she remembered the feeling of unease she'd experienced when she'd visited the woman that afternoon.

The three preschoolers Mrs. Burton was caring for had been sitting in front of the television, watching a tape of Saturday-morning cartoons and two infants had been lying in a playpen, vacantly staring at the ceiling.

Eleanore sighed. She didn't want that kind of existence for Lacey, even on a temporary basis.

The buzzing of the doorbell broke into her unhappy thoughts and she hurried to answer it before the noise woke the sleeping baby.

Swinging the door open, she blinked in surprise at the sight of the man who stood before her. She sucked in her breath and her heart stopped beating for a fraction of a second, then lurched into a slow, heavy pounding that reverberated through her entire body. For a brief moment she was catapulted back to her seventeenth summer, when she'd first seen Robert De Niro in a film; she'd had the same mindless reaction then.

Shaking her head to dispel her disorientation, she took a deep, steadying breath and said, "May I help you?"

"Yes." His husky voice with its faint foreign intonation seemed to stroke across her skin, which intensified the throbbing of her heartbeat.

His gaze skimmed over the loose curls that tumbled to her shoulders before pausing to assess the thrust of her small breasts against the thin, blue fabric of her T-shirt. To her dismay, she could feel their tips hardening in response. Finally, after what seemed like an age to her beleaguered senses, he focused his attention lower, down over the well-worn jeans that hugged her slender thighs to her bare toes.

Eleanore prodded her pride. She wasn't some impressionable teenager who didn't know the facts of life. She was a sophisticated woman of almost thirty; she could take control.

"Well, so far we've established that you want something from me," she said, trying for a light tone, "but not what."

"For the moment I'll settle for speaking to you." He calmly walked past her into the apartment.

A tremor shivered down her spine. This stranger had no right to simply waltz into her home like this. Unless . . . an unpalatable thought suddenly occurred to her. Could Kelly somehow be mixed up with this man?

On the surface, it didn't seem likely. For one thing, he appeared to be in his mid-thirties, much too old for her nineteen-year-old cousin. But on the other hand, his air of sophistication and casual arrogance would probably appeal to a naive teenager.

Uneasily, she closed the door and turned to study him, searching his face for some resemblance to Lacey. His crisp, black hair bore no similarity to Lacey's wispy brown curls. Nor did his piercing black eyes seem related to Lacey's sleepy brown ones. Nor was there any similarity between his sharp blade of a nose and Lacey's tiny upturned one. Imperceptibly, Eleanore relaxed slightly. This man couldn't possibly be Lacey's father.

"I don't believe I caught your name?" she ventured, trying to get the upper hand.

"Probably because I didn't give it."

"Well, suppose you do," she said tartly, "because I'm much too busy to waste my time playing twenty questions."

"Nineteen. You've already used one."

"Great, just what this evening needed." She threw up her hands in annoyance. "An aspirant to the borscht circuit."

"The what circuit?" he repeated blankly.

"Never mind." She sighed. "Just get on with it. Presumably you have a reason for being here. Would it be too much trouble to ask you to state it?"

"Not at all. I'm an emissary from your father."

Disappointment filled her at his words.

"Listen, mister, I don't know what my Uncle George told you, but, if he's hoping to use you to get money out of me, he must be even drunker than he normally is."

The man's eyes narrowed at her blunt words. "I am unacquainted with your Uncle George, drunk or sober. I referred to your father."

"I haven't got a father," she said, instinctively rejecting her natural father as he'd rejected her so many years before.

"An interesting biological phenomenon," he said dryly.

Eleanore bit her lip against the hot words she longed to throw at him, took a deep breath, and tried again. "Suppose we get directly to your purpose in coming here."

"I told you. I wanted to talk to you."

"So you did, but we haven't as yet established that I want to talk to you. Now, I would like to know who I'm talking to."

"Miss Fulton—"

"Your name," she repeated doggedly.

"Murad Ahiqar. As I said, I represent your father."

"Am I to assume that after nearly thirty years, my father has suddenly decided I exist?"

"He's always known you existed. He'd be hard-pressed not to, considering the amount of support he's paid over the years."

"Support?" Eleanore glared at him. "My so-called father skipped out on his responsibilities the minute my mother told him she was pregnant. The only thing he ever gave her was the advice to get an abortion."

"Who do you think paid your bills all the years you were growing up? Who paid your college tuition? Who paid your dowry?"

"In the first place, my mother sent my Aunt Theresa money for my room and board whenever she could. In the second, I paid my own college bills with a job, a scholarship and loans. And in the third, since I've never been married, what would I want with a dowry?" Her voice rose angrily on the final word. How dare this . . . this stranger barge in here and malign her poor mother. If her father had really sent money over the years then her mother would have been able to keep her. She and her mother could have been a real family and she could have had a normal home like other children. She wouldn't have been dependent on the charity of her relatives.

"Is that what your mother says?" Murad demanded.

"She can't say anything. She'd dead! She—" Eleanore broke off as Lacey, awakened by the sound of their argument, began to cry.

"What's that?" Murad's eyebrows met in a heavy frown.

"Not what, who." Eleanore hurried into the bedroom and picked up the wailing baby, taking her back into the living room. "There, there, sweet'n. It's all right. The nasty man's just leaving."

"You should have." Murad's icy voice sliced through Eleanore's flow of soothing words.

Eleanore blinked at the anger in his voice. "Should have what?"

"Should have gotten married," he said. "It would appear history really does repeat itself."

"At least Lacey's father isn't some Middle-Eastern playboy with delusions of grandeur," she shot back.

"Oh? And who is this paragon?"

"Well, I'm not sure exactly, but—" Eleanore broke off at the expression of contempt that darkened his face.

"Selim's daughter dares to admit she doesn't even know who fathered her child!"

Eleanore's mouth dropped open; he actually thought Lacey was hers. She couldn't decide whether to be amused or insulted. It was his reference to her as Selim's daughter that tipped the balance.

"My father long ago gave up the right to question what I do and with whom I do it, and you never had the right. Now, take your double standard and get out."

"I'm—"

"Either you leave or I'll scream and when the neighbors call the police, you can try explaining yourself to them."

"Perhaps you're right. At the moment, I'm much too disgusted to discuss this rationally. Good day." He gave her a curt nod and stalked from the apartment, closing the door behind him with a decided snap.

"It hasn't been so far," Eleanore muttered, sinking down on the sofa. Somehow, it seemed a fitting finale to this truly ghastly day that the sexiest man she'd ever encountered not only had ties to her despicable father, but had also jumped to an entirely erroneous conclusion about her.

Not that it really mattered. Murad Ahiqar's interest in her had been solely on her father's behalf, and that kind of interest she most definitely didn't need. She already had enough problems without the added complication of her oh-so-loving father's suddenly remembering her existence.

For a second she considered Murad's claim that her father had been sending money for her support all those years, before she dismissed it as disloyal to her mother. Besides, she decided on a more practical note, if Selim had really cared enough to support her, he'd have also cared enough to have found out something about her. With the financial resources that appeared to be at his command, it wouldn't have been difficult. And if he'd seen the precarious nature of her upbringing, he would have changed it. Even if the change had been nothing more than the relative stability of a good boarding school.

No, she concluded. For some reason, Selim had decided he wanted to see her and was lying to whitewash his previous indifference. But all the lies in the world couldn't change the past. It was over. The time to know her father had been twenty-five years ago when she'd ached for a family of her own. Now, she had no interest in her father. Or in his arrogant emissary. Resolutely banishing Murad's dark features from her thoughts, she smiled down at Lacey.

"Tell me, my pet, shall we take the good baby-sitter and cut back on eating?"

Lacey gurgled happily.

"That's what I thought, too." Eleanore kissed the baby's downy head. "Let's get your bottle heated up."

2

"ELEANORE! Wait for me." Liz sprinted across the lobby for the elevator Eleanore obligingly held for her.

"Thanks," Liz panted. "It takes forever for this thing to come back down. How's the world's cutest baby?" She rubbed her forefinger along Lacey's soft cheek and received a drooling smile in return.

"Missing her mother." Eleanore punched the button for the eleventh floor. "The poor lamb can't seem to sleep more than two hours at a stretch."

"Poor you." Liz eyed her critically. "You look like you've lost weight these past two weeks and you didn't have any to spare. Forgive me if I point out that you look like hell."

Eleanore chuckled. "What are friends for?"

"For lending you money."

"I appreciate the thought, but I'll get by. I substituted two days last week and three days this week." She made an effort to sound positive. "Things are looking up."

"Have you located Kelly?"

"No. I've checked with all her friends. No one's seen her."

"Or they simply aren't telling you." Liz held the elevator doors open on the eleventh floor.

"I considered that, but Kelly's friends aren't particularly loyal."

"Like Kelly herself," Liz said scathingly. "Eleanore, how long are you going to allow your family to use you like this?"

Eleanore shifted the sleepy baby and unlocked her apartment door. "They aren't taking anything I'm not willing to give. Quit painting me as some kind of martyr."

"I was thinking more along the lines of a victim." Liz followed her into the apartment. "Lady, Cinderella had nothing on you."

"She had Prince Charming." Eleanore laughed and went to put Lacey in her crib.

"That's what you need," Liz announced the second Eleanore returned to the living room.

Eleanore blinked. "Prince Charming? Sorry, blond men with blue eyes never appealed to me." But dark men . . . Unbidden, a picture of Murad Ahiqar popped full-blown into her mind. His ebony hair was slightly tousled and his black eyes gleamed with laughter instead of anger. She immediately rejected the image. He wasn't the least bit charming. Or if he was, he hadn't wasted any charm on her. But much more annoying than his brusque manner was the fact that he'd lied. Her heart started to pound at the thought of his ridiculous claim that her father had paid support for her.

"No, not Prince Charming." Liz's pensive voice cut into Eleanore's angry thoughts. "You need a rich husband to take all your financial worries off your shoulders."

"Any woman stupid enough to marry a man for his money deserves everything she gets, and I don't mean that in a positive sense. Besides, the whole question is moot. If you added together the total financial worth of every male I've ever dated, it still wouldn't equal one wealthy man."

"There is that. But I still like the idea."

"I think I'll simply muddle along on my own until Kelly comes back." Fear tightened her voice. "I mean, how long can it take for her to find herself?"

"Since there doesn't appear to be any substance to your cousin, she could spend her whole life looking and never find anything."

"You're a great comfort."

"I'm practical." Liz got to her feet. "Life's much easier if you see people as they are, instead of as you want them to be."

Liz was wrong, Eleanore thought as she locked the door behind her friend. She didn't have any illusions about Kelly. She knew exactly what her cousin was, but simply because she knew Kelly's faults didn't mean that she didn't love her just the same. When all was said and done, Kelly and Lacey were her family.

Again, the image of Murad's dark face floated through her mind, reminding her of yet another member of her family who after a silence of nearly thirty years was demanding recognition. Eleanore shifted restlessly under the memory of the searing contempt in his emissary's ebony eyes.

She couldn't help wishing that she'd met Murad Ahiqar under more normal circumstances. And when would a schoolteacher have met someone like him, she mocked herself, remembering the pitifully few facts she'd been able to uncover about him from her research in the periodical section of the public library. The primary one being that he was wealthy beyond the dreams of avarice. He belonged to an entirely different world than she did. A world that would never have impinged on hers if it hadn't been for her father's quixotic desire to see her. A desire that appeared to have died once Murad told him she was leading such an irresponsible life she couldn't even name the father of her child.

Ah, well, she had better things to worry about than her father's perfidy—headed by the precarious state of her finances. She'd only worked five days these past two weeks. After she paid the baby-sitter and the electricity and phone bills, there would be barely enough money left to buy food. She consoled herself with the thought that at least she had her savings to fall back on for rent.

"Here is the report you've been waiting for, Your Excellency. Colonel Saleizad just delivered it."

"Thank you, Ali. That'll be all." Murad placed the manila folder down in the middle of his huge, mahogany desk, opened it and began to read. As he progressed, his expression grew grimmer and a muscle at the corner of his mouth began to twitch angrily.

"Of all the tangled, stupid . . ." He raked his fingers through his hair. Selim must have been out of his mind to have blindly sent money to that woman for all those years without ever once having bothered to check that it was actually being spent on his daughter.

Murad snorted in disgust. According to this report, Selim's trust had been badly misplaced. Instead of caring for Eleanore, Marilyn had dumped the child on her long-suffering sister and left poor Theresa to raise her with no more than occasional token help.

Eleanore had been telling the truth about how she'd paid for her college education. While her mother had been living it up on the French Riviera with the money Selim had sent for her tuition fees, Eleanore had been working in an insurance office to make ends meet.

Murad reread the beginning of the third page, frowning thoughtfully as he considered the information. So the baby was her cousin's. But why would Eleanore claim her?

He stared out the window at the large walled garden, trying to recall exactly what had happened. A grimace of self-disgust twisted his lips. Eleanore hadn't said the baby was hers. He'd leaped to that conclusion all by himself. She simply hadn't bothered to correct him.

She certainly had a temper. Murad felt his blood quicken at the memory of her sparkling eyes and the warm flush that had tinted the creamy perfection of her ivory skin. He wondered if she would be as passionate in bed as she was in anger. Reluctantly, he squashed his curiosity; tempting though the idea of finding out was, he knew it was a bad one. Becoming romantically involved with Eleanore would add far too many complications to an already overly complicated situation. At the moment, he appeared to be the only objective person among them; it would be best for all concerned if he remained so.

He frowned as he began to read the detailed account of her financial situation. According to these figures, at the rate she was draining her reserves, she'd be unable to meet her rent payments in five months—sooner if she met unexpected expenses.

At least that was one problem that Selim's money could easily solve, and, as his daughter, Eleanore had every right to his help. Murad glanced at his watch. It would be nearly eleven by the time he could get to her apartment. A little late to be calling, but he found himself unable to resist the impulse to see her tonight.

"GO TO SLEEP, little baby, because if you don't I'm going to start crying along with you." Eleanore sang in a soothing monotone, until, to her infinite relief, Lacey finally fell asleep and Eleanore was able to put her in her crib.

11:05, the clock read. If she was lucky, Lacey wouldn't wake for several hours. Eleanore rubbed her aching forehead. What she wouldn't give for eight hours of uninterrupted sleep.

The doorbell rang, echoing loudly in the silent apartment.

"Oh, no!" She rushed to answer it before the noise woke up Lacey and she started crying again.

Making sure the latch was on, Eleanore opened the door a crack and peered out into the shadowy hallway. Her heart skipped a beat and then sped up as she recognized Murad. To her surprise, his expression seemed almost indulgent.

She straightened her shoulders. It didn't matter what his mood was, this man was a danger to her peace of mind. Every instinct for self-preservation she possessed was telling her to get rid of him.

"Unlatch the door and let me in." His deep, velvet voice slid over her receptive senses, heightening her awareness of him.

"No," she said bluntly, watching in fascination as his eyes widened in disbelief. Now that was interesting, she thought. Apparently, he didn't get many flat refusals to his orders.

"I wish to talk to you and I would prefer to do it in the privacy of your apartment." His measured tones did not reflect the annoyance she could see shimmering in his eyes.

"Not only is it much too late for social chitchat but I've finally got the baby to sleep and I want to go to bed."

"You'll sleep better once we've talked."

Eleanore mentally rejected his claim; she found any exposure to him unsettling in the extreme. "Maybe later in the week."

"Either you open the door or I'll put my finger on the bell and leave it there until the baby wakes up." His threat was delivered in a perfectly pleasant tone of voice that infuriated her. Of all the arrogant, pigheaded males!

"All right, you can have ten minutes, that's all. It's too late to entertain." She unlatched the door and swung it open.

"There can be no impropriety in your letting me in. Our fathers have been friends for over forty years."

"Where exactly are you and my father from?" she asked, curious about Murad's faint accent.

"Abar. It's a small kingdom on the Persian Gulf." At her blank look he added, "You will be seeing it yourself, soon."

"I will?" She eyed him narrowly. "How do you figure that?"

"Your father lives there and when you visit him—"

"My father's arrogance is unbelievable!" Eleanore snapped. "He's ignored my existence for twenty-nine years, and then out of a clear blue sky, he decides he'd like to meet me. But does he bother to look me up himself? Oh, no. He sends someone to fetch me like a stray package. Unless, of course, he's physically incapacitated in some way?" She glanced questioningly at Murad.

"No, and in the interest of accuracy, he didn't send me to fetch you. I was coming to New York on business anyway."

"Ah, yes. I saw a picture of your . . . business on the front page of a scandal sheet in the grocery store today. If that's a sample of what you consider work, I wonder what you do for fun. Ah—" Eleanore grinned at his annoyed expression "—did I hit a nerve?"

"Baiting me will get you absolutely nowhere."

"I don't know about that. It's doing wonders for my mental health."

"This is getting us nowhere," Murad said in exasperation.

"I already am where I want to be. Will you quit hovering and sit down." Eleanore waved toward the couch. Despite the fact that he couldn't have been taller than five-ten, his physical presence seemed to dominate the small room. She hoped that once he was seated the effect would be diminished.

"I can hardly sit while you remain standing."

"Oh?" Eleanore blinked, surprised at his old-world manners. But then he *was* from another world, she reminded herself, a fact that his flawless command of the English language tended to obscure. She sat down in a chair, ignoring his sardonic glance at her transparent attempt to avoid sitting beside him on the sofa. She was already far too aware of him. Sitting close to him would only intensify the problem.

"Are you afraid of me, Eleanore?" He eyed her narrowly.

"No. Like any good hostess, I'm concerned for your safety."

He blinked in surprise. "My safety?"

"Uh-huh. As maddening as you are, I'm liable to give in to an impulse to give you a good, swift kick in the shins. Over here, I can't reach you, so you're safe."

"I think I'm safe, period. You couldn't hurt a flea."

"Could too," she retorted and then bit her tongue in frustration. Of all the juvenile retorts! Taking a deep breath, she tried to gain control of the situation.

"This whole discussion is not only irrelevant, it's used up almost half your allotted ten minutes. Not that it matters, since it's going to take me considerably less time than that to conclude our business. You simply tell Selim that I respectfully decline the privilege of traveling halfway across the world to be looked over to see if I'm fit to be acknowledged as his daughter."

"There's no question of his refusing to acknowledge you. He's always supported you. It wasn't his fault that your mother dumped you on her sister and spent the money on herself."

"He's a liar!" Eleanore argued. "I told you before there was no money. There never was. He's simply trying to make it seem that my mother was the villain of the piece now that she's dead and no longer able to defend herself."

"I can show you canceled checks—"

"Credit me with more sense than that," she said scathingly. "I know half a dozen places in New York City where, for a hundred bucks, I can get forged checks proving that I paid *him* money all those years. He could have easily done the same."

"This is totally unproductive," Murad said, wondering why she kept insisting her mother was dead when he knew for a fact that Marilyn was not only alive, but living in California.

"I could have told you that. As a matter of fact, I did. Right before I gave you my final word on the subject. Would you please leave now?" she added when he didn't move.

"I promised Selim I'd send you to him."

"Tough. Go back and tell him that his daughter has decided to take a leaf out of his book and ignore him for the next thirty years. Besides, somehow I can't believe he's not having second thoughts about acknowledging me now that he knows that I made him a grandfather without benefit of marriage."

What was she up to? Why didn't she correct his original assumption that the baby was hers? And not only wasn't she correcting it, but she was deliberately embellishing it. Unless she was trying to use the baby to keep her father at a distance? It was impossible for him to tell and he doubted if she herself really knew. She'd hated her father for so long that her rejection of him seemed to be instinctive. It was not going to be easy to get her to see Selim as the kind, gentle man Murad knew him to be. In fact, at this moment it appeared to be an impossible task, but he was much too fond of Selim not to try.

"Selim is a good man," he began. "He was like a second father to me when I was growing up."

A corrosive bitterness filled Eleanore. Selim had abandoned her without a thought and yet he'd been willing to be a surrogate father to an old friend's son. It all seemed so unfair.

Her resentment spilled over. "Well, he didn't raise *me*."

"Your father—"

"Don't keep calling him that. He isn't. Not in any way that counts. He excluded me from his life before I was even born. Tell him to be satisfied with you."

"Your father did you a great wrong," Murad admitted. "He should have told Amineh what had happened and taken you to Abar with him."

"My mother would have had something to say about that," Eleanore snapped.

"Considering that she left you with your aunt, I doubt it. But the past is over and can't be changed. Your future is what concerns Selim."

"There is no future for my father and me," she insisted. "Besides, even if I were stupid enough to go to Abar, what's to stop him from taking one look at me and saying, 'Sorry, I've changed my mind again. Go home.' Or, more likely, to welcome me and in a few months, when the novelty of having a daughter has worn off, change his mind yet again."

"Your place in the family—"

"Was usurped by you," Eleanore said flatly. "As you so succinctly pointed out, the past can't be changed." She rubbed her throbbing head in an unconsciously revealing gesture. This whole discussion was all so pointless. And petty, she admitted shamefully. She had no right to vent her own long-buried bitterness at her father's desertion on Murad. It wasn't his fault that Selim had preferred him to her. Nor did it make any difference. Not now. Now she was a grown woman with her own life to live.

"Listen to me, Murad. I—" she broke off as Lacey woke with a piercing howl.

"Oh, no!" Eleanore closed her eyes against an urge to burst into self-pitying tears. It would take hours to get Lacey back to sleep. And not only that but she still had Murad camped in her living room, refusing to take no for an answer. She gave him a frustrated glare and hurried into the nursery.

Murad rubbed the side of his nose, thinking and listening to the soft crooning sounds Eleanore made as she tried to soothe the obviously unhappy baby.

The melodic sound of her voice slipped through his mind, heightening his awareness of her. His palms began to tingle as he remembered the proud thrust of her small breasts against her soft sweater. He shifted restlessly as he imagined her without the concealment of clothes. She was like a gazelle—soft, sleek and graceful. There was something about her....

He shook his head. What there was was probably nothing more than plain old sexual attraction. It was simply a much more potent variety than he'd run across before. Besides, even if he did find her intriguing, she most definitely wasn't interested in him. He'd roused her animosity the minute he'd mentioned Selim. And not without justification, he admitted. Eleanore had been treated abominably by the two people who should have protected her. But that was in the past. The present was what concerned him. And right at this moment, Eleanore desperately needed financial help. The question was, how to give it to her without offending her prickly pride. And equally important, how to reconcile her with Selim so that her aunt's family couldn't continue to use her in the future.

He considered various possibilities. She wouldn't take money, but suppose he could convince her to be his houseguest for a few months? That would alleviate her immediate financial worries and at the same time give him some measure of control over a highly volatile situation.

"Come on, sweetheart." Eleanore carried the baby into the living room. "Let's warm you a bottle. I—" She broke off as she saw Murad.

"Haven't you left yet?"

"No. I have a proposition for you. I'd like you to be my houseguest for a while."

"What?" She ignored the surge of excitement that followed in the wake of his offer in favor of finding out why he'd made it. From what she'd read in the scandal sheets, Murad Ahiqar was a confirmed hedonist, not a casual do-gooder. "I think I missed something. You're inviting me to move into your apartment—"

"House," he corrected. "I have a four-storied town house over on 58th Street near Sutton Place. My staff will be perfectly adequate chaperons, if that's what you're worried about."

"Modern women don't worry about things like that. They learn judo instead." She wondered if he saw her as a sex-starved spinster who thought every man she met had designs on her virtue. It was a depressing thought. "But that's not what I'm getting at. What I don't understand is why you'd put up with having a houseguest. Especially one who comes with an infant."

"I think we can be of benefit to each other," he said with seeming casualness. "On my side I've got two major problems. Your father—" he ignored the way her lips tightened "—is Abar's oil minister and he's supposed to be mapping out strategy for a very important OPEC meeting at the end of the month. Instead, his mind is taken up with trying to get me to arrange a meeting with you. I'd expect you to agree to meet him so that he can turn his attention back to his work."

"Simply meet him?"

"With an open mind," he amended.

"I'd need a vacant mind to forget what he's done," Eleanore retorted. "You said you had two problems. What's the other?" She wondered if the blonde in the newspaper photos with him was becoming too demanding and he was looking for another woman to use as a smoke screen. She wasn't certain even in her own mind whether she was disappointed or not when his problem turned out to be something entirely different.

"Last month my father decided that it was time I became involved in our family's business concerns, so he sent me here to take charge of our American investment company. Unfortunately, I'm having a little trouble relating to my employees."

"I can imagine," she said dryly.

"So I thought that if I were to hold a series of social functions over the next two months and you were there to act as my hostess—"

"Why not use the blonde who was decorating the front page of the newspaper with you?" she probed, intensely curious about the woman.

"Sonia? I imagine my office staff would have even less in common with her than they do with me." His amused chuckle grated on Eleanore's nerves. "No, you'd be perfect. I can pass you off as a friend of the family, and with your middle-class American background you'd fit right in."

He was probably right, she realized.

"And since you're out of work..."

"How did you know that?" she asked suspiciously.

"I spoke to a little old lady in the elevator the first time I was here, and she mentioned what a shame it was that you'd been laid off." Murad lied without a blink, knowing that to admit he'd had her investigated would ruin everything.

"A little old lady?"

"A Mrs. Benton, I believe she said her name was." He pulled the name of her next-door neighbor out of his memory.

That sounded like her garrulous neighbor, Eleanore thought. Carefully, she considered his unexpected offer. If she were living in his house, then her only expense would be her rent. She wouldn't have to worry about paying the gas, electric or phone bills. Nor would she have to buy food or pay a baby-sitter. She'd be able to take care of Lacey herself.

And not only that, but playing the part of his hostess in the evenings would leave her days free to search for Kelly. But there was another factor involved, she admitted with her usual lack of self-deception. Her unexpected and totally inexplicable attraction to Murad. No, not attraction; attraction was such a lukewarm word. The emotion Murad raised in her was much too intense to be called mere attraction.

The feeling reminded her of something that had happened one summer a few years ago when she'd been on vacation in Wyoming. Lightning had started a devastating forest fire that was clearly visible from the park lodge where she'd been staying. She remembered standing on the edge of the parking lot and watching the primitive beauty of the brilliant orange-red flames lighting the night sky. Even knowing how very dangerous those flames were, she'd still felt drawn to them. Drawn to go a little closer. To reach out to them.

The emotion Murad raised in her was like that fire—elemental, out of control and very, very dangerous. But it was also very rare. In all her adult life she'd only once felt anything that even vaguely approximated it, and that had been no more than a teenage infatuation with an image on a movie screen. It hadn't survived seeing the person in the flesh.

Maybe the feeling Murad engendered wouldn't last either. Maybe it would fade if she came into daily contact with him. All she knew for certain was that if she didn't find out, she'd always wonder what might have happened. She shot a quick glance at him, wondering if her feelings were reciprocated on any level. It was impossible to tell. His face didn't give anything away, although several times she had caught brief flashes of some emotion in his black eyes. But that could easily have been exasperation because she wouldn't agree to meet her father.

She sighed. She wanted to accept his offer, and not simply because of the very compelling financial benefits. She wanted to accept because she was intensely curious about the man who'd made the offer.

But what did she really know about him? She nervously chewed her lip. Suppose, despite his denials, once he had her in his house he pounced? Her common sense quickly made a mockery of that idea. In the first place, Murad represented her father, a man for whom he obviously had a great deal of respect and affection. And, judging from the scandal sheet she'd read, Murad most assuredly wasn't starved for affection. In fact, he was presently feeding his male ego with a much more exotic feminine dish than she could ever hope to be. No matter which angle she looked at it from, his offer had undoubtedly been made for exactly the reasons he'd stated. He stood to gain as much from the arrangement as she did. Making up her mind, she said, "I accept."

"Good." A brief smile lit his face, suddenly making him seem younger and much more approachable. "I'll send a car for you tomorrow evening. Say about six?"

"Six is fine," she said absently, her attention focused on the dimple in his left cheek that his smile had brought to life.

"Until tomorrow then." He lightly flicked the tip of her nose with a fingertip.

Eleanore's eyes widened at the sparks that danced over her skin, and she rubbed her still-tingling flesh while watching him leave. Whatever it was that Murad had, it was certainly potent.

3

"HERE, TAKE THIS." Liz shoved a covered dish at Eleanore the second she opened her apartment door.

Eleanore automatically accepted it. "What is it?"

"Dessert for your dinner. I've got the main course here." She gestured with a foil-covered pan she was carrying in her other hand. "My group-therapy class at the prison is exploring self-expression through cooking and these are the leftovers."

"No, thank you." Eleanore followed Liz into the tiny kitchen. "If I remember correctly, that group is made up of violent offenders. *Multiple* violent offenders. Their kind of self-expression could kill a person."

"Don't be silly." Liz looked around for a free surface to set the pan down. She couldn't find one; there were boxes everywhere. "We made this in the prison's kitchens. There aren't any poisons around."

"That's what you think. The ancient Japanese used to commit suicide by eating a pound of salt."

"Really?" Liz glanced speculatively at the dish in her hand. "Naw. No one could eat that much salt without knowing it." Opening the refrigerator, she shoved the casserole inside and then demanded, "What's going on around here?"

"I'm packing." Eleanore sealed the box she had been working on.

"Packing! But why? I told you I'd lend you money."

"And I told you it isn't necessary, and it isn't. I've found an alternative. It's a live-in job."

"Doing what?"

"Acting as a sort of hostess. It's a long story."

"On the contrary, it sounds all too short. And familiar. Have you gotten yourself mixed up with a man?"

"That rather depends on what you mean by 'mixed up.' Hand me one of those empty boxes behind you, would you?"

Liz gave her one and then prodded, "So, tell me."

"I did. I was offered a job of sorts and I accepted."

"It's the 'of sorts' part that bothers me! Where did you meet this guy?"

"Here. He came to the apartment. Twice, as a matter of fact."

"And he just happened to have this job opening at the exact time that you needed one?"

"Of course he didn't," Eleanore muttered, her attention centered on her packing.

"Then why did he offer to let you move in with him?"

"Because, my dear Sherlock, he has an ulterior motive." Eleanore grinned at her.

"I knew it!"

"Not that!"

"All men have *that* as a motive."

"You, my friend, are in imminent danger of becoming a cynic." Eleanore carefully wrapped a china figurine in paper.

"Will you stop that damned packing and talk to me?"

"I can't. I promised Mr. Petrocini I'd have the apartment cleared by six."

"What does our custodian have to do with this?"

"Well, when I went down yesterday to tell him I'd be living elsewhere for a few months and to ask him to keep an eye on things for me, he asked if I'd let him sublet my apartment while I was gone. It seems that his is being remodeled and his wife wants to get away from the mess. It's a perfect setup," Eleanore said enthusiastically. "Not only won't I have any expenses, but since he and his wife only need one bedroom, they said I could store all my stuff in Lacey's room."

"Bills could be the least of your worries," Liz said ominously.

Eleanore gave her friend an amused glance. "Here, let me show you something." She rummaged through the stack of papers on the counter and, finding the one she wanted, handed it to Liz. "Take a look at that."

"'Alien invaders make ninety-year-old woman pregnant'?" Liz read.

"Not the headline! The picture."

"Two gorgeous people with more money than common sense. So?"

"So, he's the man who offered me the job."

"What?"

"Uh-huh. And believe me, men who date women who look like that aren't going to try to trap their houseguests in dark corners." Her voice was almost wistful.

"Be grateful," Liz said tartly. "From the looks of it, the guy is way out of your league. But I still don't like it. What is his ulterior motive?"

"Don't worry, it's not sexual. But I'd really rather not talk about it," Eleanore said. Much as she liked Liz, she didn't want to discuss her father's sudden appearance in her life. She needed time to get used to the idea first.

"All right." Liz threw up her hands in defeat. "No more lectures. Just remember, if you should need a bolt hole, my couch is all yours. Tell me, have you heard from Kelly?"

Eleanore grimaced. "The silence is deafening. I've called all her friends at least twice. No one will admit to even seeing her. It's as if she's simply slipped off the edge of the world."

"I hate to mention this, but . . ." Liz hesitated.

"Foul play? I already checked with the police department and the hospitals. It was negative."

"Thank heavens for that."

"Quite." Eleanore went back to her packing.

"Well, if I can't change your mind, at least I can help you. You say you want these boxes in Lacey's bedroom?"

"Uh-huh. Thanks, Liz."

"What are friends for?" Liz picked up a box. "Where will you be living?"

"Sutton Place, near 58th."

Liz whistled. "At least you'll get to see how the other half lives. What'd you say this guy's name was?"

"Murad Ahiqar."

"Arab?"

"He's from a small country on the gulf called Abar."

"I take it his money comes from oil?"

"I assume so."

"I still don't like it," Liz muttered as she carried the box out.

And Liz would like it even less if she knew just how attractive she found Murad Ahiqar, Eleanore thought ruefully. Not that she had any intention of telling her friend. Her response to Murad was intensely private, a secret that she wanted to hug to herself.

But what happened if her reaction to Murad did last? For the first time she considered the ramifications. What if it not only lasted, but deepened into something like love? A sudden doubt about the wisdom of becoming his houseguest shook her. She might be optimistic by nature, but it would take a Pollyanna to manufacture a happy ending out of that scenario.

It didn't matter, she told herself, trying hard to believe it. She was an adult, able to handle whatever happened. What she might find harder to handle would be the might-have-beens that would nag her for the rest of her life if she didn't at least explore her feelings.

Resolutely, she turned back to her packing.

By five forty-five, Eleanore was feeling decidedly the worse for wear. She was physically tired and emotionally strung out. She would have preferred hiding in the closet to facing a strange household.

She grimaced as she studied her tense features in the bedroom mirror. She looked every bit as apprehensive as she felt. Taking out her makeup kit, she carefully smoothed on eye shadow, added blush to her pale cheeks and outlined her lips in a ripe cherry red. Critically, she studied her hair, which fell in loose curls to her shoulders, wondering whether she should put it up in a chignon, as she did when she was teaching, or leave it as it was. The chime of her alarm warning her that her transportation would arrive in fifteen minutes decided her. She didn't have time to restyle her hair. She still had to get Lacey ready.

Eleanore hurriedly zipped the grumbling baby into a clean pink sleeper. "Just hang in there a little longer, angel." She kissed Lacey's soft cheek.

She paused as the doorbell rang, echoing loudly through the denuded apartment. Assuming it was the driver of the car Murad had promised, Eleanore opened the door to find Murad himself standing in the hallway. Her startled gaze took in his white tucked shirt and faultlessly tailored dinner jacket. He looked elegant, sophisticated and totally out of place in her middle-class apartment building.

"It must be true," he said.

"What?"

"That clothes make the man." He chuckled. "I'm just not sure from the expression on your face what they made me into."

"I was simply surprised to see you," Eleanore said, attempting to excuse her gauche behavior. She stepped back so he could enter, trying to ignore the sinking feeling in the pit of her stomach. Had he changed his mind about his offer? Was that why he'd come himself?

She went straight to the heart of the matter. "Why are you here?"

"To take you home."

"I didn't realize it was a formal occasion," she quipped, hoping the relief she was feeling wasn't showing in her eyes.

"I have a dinner engagement this evening," he said.

Well, that answered her question about whether or not her feelings were reciprocated, she thought ruefully. Ah, well, at least she'd be able to relax and unpack without the added burden of having to cope with her unsettling host.

"I wanted to apprise you of a few facts. Please sit down."

"No, thanks. Lacey's only happy as long as I keep moving."

Murad frowned. "That hardly seems normal."

"How would you know?" she asked without rancor.

"Quite easily. I have thirteen nieces and nephews and they all started out as infants."

"*No!*" Eleanore gave him a glance of wide-eyed wonder. "How obliging of them."

"I'm sure their mothers thought so." He grinned at her.

"Quite," she muttered, deciding it was time to change the subject. "What about these facts you mentioned?"

"The most important one is Miss Kelvington."

"Miss Kelvington?" Eleanore's mind flew to the blonde who had shared the front page of the scandal sheet with Murad. Hadn't that woman's name been Sonia something-or-other?

"Lacey's nanny."

"Lacey's what?"

"Nanny," Murad repeated calmly. "I hired a nanny for her. Miss Kelvington comes highly recommended by the French ambassador to the United Nations. His youngest went back to France to boarding school this fall, so Miss Kelvington's services were no longer needed. And since the new baby she'd be looking after won't be born until January, she's agreed to take care of Lacey for the next few months."

Eleanore wondered grimly if this paragon would be so agreeable when she found out that she couldn't afford to pay her. Nannies didn't come cheap, especially the variety who looked after ambassadors' kids.

"I don't need a nanny," she said tightly.

"She's not for you, she's for Lacey."

Murad's grin infuriated her. How could he be cracking jokes—and bad ones at that—when she was worried sick about the whole situation? "Don't you feel you've been just the slightest bit presumptuous, hiring a nanny without consulting me?"

"No," he said simply.

"You, sir, are an autocrat of the first order."

"Wait till you meet my father," Murad said. "Now, there's an autocrat. When I was a kid, I used to think he was exactly like the Queen of Hearts in *Alice in Wonderland*."

"Lovely, something to look forward to." Eleanore sighed. "But about this nanny. . ."

"Miss Kelvington. She has fantastic credentials."

"I don't care if she's Mother Theresa. I don't want her. I'm perfectly capable of looking after one small baby."

"With very big lungs," he added. "But your capabilities aren't in question. It's your ability to be in two places at once that is."

"What?" Eleanore frowned in confusion.

"You agreed to act as my hostess. You can't do that if you have to be constantly running up to the nursery to comfort a crying baby. The only alternative I can see is to let the poor little thing scream. You can hardly prefer that."

"No." Eleanore closed her eyes in defeat. There was no help for it. She'd have to come right out and tell him she couldn't afford a nanny even for a few months. The words burned like acid on her tongue. She hadn't wanted him to know just how precarious her financial position really was.

Taking a deep breath, she said bluntly, "Paying this Miss Kelvington's salary would probably leave me penniless."

"You aren't being asked to. Her salary is my responsibility."

"I won't take your charity!" Living in his house was one thing, but having him feel he had to spend money on her offended her pride.

"It isn't charity."

"Yes, it is."

"Think for a minute. You agreed to act as my hostess. I hardly expect you to be out of pocket because of our arrangement. An arrangement, I might add, that will pay me handsome dividends in terms of future office harmony. Believe me, the cost of Lacey's nanny and a few dresses are negligible in comparison."

"What's wrong with my clothes?" she demanded, sensing criticism of her taste.

"Nothing." He studied her cream wool suit with obvious approval, soothing her ruffled sensibilities. "But I doubt you have many evening clothes, and that's when we'll be doing most of our entertaining."

"I see," she said slowly, realizing that he was right. Her evening wear would never pass muster in his circles.

"What you say makes sense," she conceded.

"Of course it does."

His smugly satisfied smile infuriated her. Confused, she studied his lean face. How could she still feel that insidious tug of attraction when she was so annoyed at him? It didn't seem to make any sense. Ah, well, she shelved her speculation, nothing about Murad had followed the rules yet.

Picking up the suitcase and diaper bag, he looked around for more. "Is this all you're taking?"

"The janitor volunteered to bring the rest of my stuff by tomorrow."

"Fine, then let's go." He ushered her out of the apartment. "By the way, I told my staff that Lacey is your niece. It would be best if you continued the fiction. They're Abarian and very conservative. Except, of course, for Wilkerson, but he's only borrowed."

"Wilkerson?"

"My butler."

"Butler!" Her eyes widened. "You have a butler?"

"Uh-huh." Murad held the elevator door for her. "He's necessary," he added cryptically.

Eleanore clutched the baby a little closer, wondering what on earth she was getting herself into.

What she was getting into was luxury on a grand scale, she realized some thirty minutes later as she looked around the enormous reception hall of Murad's home. A thick Oriental carpet in blue and cream covered the Italian marble floor and an enormous Venetian-crystal chandelier showered prisms of rainbow-hued light over everything.

Eleanore shivered slightly, finding such elegance vaguely intimidating.

Murad caught her unease. "What's wrong?"

"Nothing," she said brightly. "You have a fantastic home."

"But you don't like it?" he persisted.

"No, it's not that. It's just that it's so...so far removed from what I'm used to. It's a good thing Lacey isn't a toddler. I shudder to think of the damage an inquisitive child could cause."

"My mother did, too, every year when my father would bring the whole family to New York for the opening session of the United Nations." Murad chuckled. "In fact, after the Battle of Waterloo, she had all the breakables stored."

"The Battle of Waterloo?" Eleanore watched in fascination as his firm lips lifted in a reminiscent smile.

"Uh-huh. My second eldest brother, Karim, is a French-history buff and one boring afternoon toward the end of our stay, we decided to enliven things by reenacting the Battle of Waterloo. Since I was the youngest, I had to be the English."

"At least you got to win."

"You don't know my brother. Historical accuracy never bothered him. So I decided to lengthen the odds in my favor. While he was mustering his troops in the study, I took the antique cannon that used to be on the third-floor landing and stuffed it full of fireworks left over from the Fourth-of-July celebration. Then, when Selim led the cavalry charge up the stairs, I fired it over their heads. It was a glorious sight. The walls and ceiling burning. My mother having hysterics. My father yelling at the top of his lungs."

Eleanore laughed. "And I thought my students were bad." Somehow his tale made him seem more human. She found it much easier to identify with a small boy who defended the stairs with a cannon than a multimillionaire whose life-style was totally alien to her. "What happened?"

"After the fire department put out the flames, and my father had made sure we were all right, he grounded us for the rest of the summer."

"Ah, Ali." Murad turned to the elderly man who had suddenly materialized from the back of the hallway. "This is Miss Fulton and her niece, Lacey. Eleanore, this is Ali, my secretary. If you need anything, ask him."

"Hello." Eleanore nodded, faintly intimidated by the man's harshly carved features. That feeling faded when he smiled warmly at the baby.

"Good evening, Miss Fulton. It's a pleasure to have a child in the house again. Even if it is only temporary." He shot a reproachful glance at Murad.

Ignoring the look, Murad looked at his watch and frowned. "Damn! I'm going to be late. Ali, call Sonia Levingham and tell her I'm on my way."

So his date was with that vacuous-looking blonde, Eleanore realized with a faint feeling of pique.

"But first show Miss Fulton to her room and introduce her to Miss Kelvington." Murad frowned at the look of displeasure on Ali's face.

"What's wrong?" Murad demanded.

"That woman has offended Gaston."

"She criticized his cooking?"

"She inspected his kitchen to make sure it was clean enough to prepare the baby's food."

Murad opened his mouth, closed it and finally asked, "Was it?"

"Certainly." Ali seemed to swell with outrage. "Gaston threatened to quit, but I was able to soothe him by pointing out that Miss Kelvington would only be here for a few months."

"And that calmed him down?"

"That and the promise of a hefty bonus," Ali said slyly.

"Sorry." Eleanore felt obligated to apologize for all the trouble her advent had caused.

"Why?" Murad casually brushed his knuckles across her cheekbone and Eleanore clenched her teeth against the surge of sensation that washed over her skin. "You weren't the one who hired Miss Kelvington. Besides, Gaston will survive. He knows which side his bread is buttered on."

She watched Murad leave and then turned back to Ali.

"If you'll come with me, Miss Fulton, I'll show you to the nursery."

"Thank you." Eleanore followed him up the stairs, feeling like a bit actress who'd suddenly been thrown into the lead role without having had a chance to study the script.

Her first sight of Miss Kelvington came as a distinct shock. She wasn't exactly sure what she'd been expecting, but a gorgeous blonde with a voluptuous figure wasn't it. She wondered in annoyance if Murad's apparent preference for blondes extended even into his staff.

"That will be all, Ali," Miss Kelvington said, dismissing him once he'd performed the introductions.

Ali glanced speculatively at Eleanore as if unsure whether or not to abandon her to the nanny's tender mercies. Finally, with an apologetic smile, he left.

"Is something the matter, madam?" Miss Kelvington's glorious green eyes hadn't missed Eleanore's flicker of emotion when she'd first caught sight of her.

"No," Eleanore lied. "Of course not." It was hardly Miss Kelvington's fault that Murad seemed to prove the truth of the old saying that gentlemen preferred blondes. "I appreciate your helping us out for a few months."

Miss Kelvington regally nodded her immaculately coiffed head. "And this, of course, is Lacey." She studied the baby in Eleanore's arms, then went on, "Now then, as to particulars. I have two full and two half days off a week as well as two evenings. I stayed in this evening to meet you, but normally Wednesday is one of my nights off. I like a midweek break."

"Wednesday?" The word jolted Eleanore. "Good Lord, it is Wednesday, isn't it!"

"And has been all day long," Miss Kelvington joked ponderously.

Eleanore smiled perfunctorily as she considered the situation. Wednesday was her evening for tutoring non-readers at her local Y's Literacy Program. She'd been so frantically busy today that it had entirely slipped her mind. She frowned, knowing she couldn't skip her session tonight. Not after having had to cancel on such short notice last week when Lacey had suddenly developed a fever.

Kathy, the young woman she was working with, had a very poor self-image. She'd be sure to interpret a second cancellation in as many weeks as a personal rejection.

Eleanore glanced at her watch. If she hurried, she could unpack and still have time to give Lacey her evening bottle before she had to leave.

"I have to go out this evening, but of course, there will be no problem about arranging your preferred time off," Eleanore said, intending to explain the situation to her student and ask her to reschedule her regular session to another evening, or better yet, to sometime during the day. Eleanore's spirits rose as she remembered that she no longer had to cram all her activities into the evening hours.

"If you'll let me know when Lacey wakes up, Miss Kelvington, I'd like to give her her evening bottle."

"Certainly, Miss Fulton."

Eleanore was tempted to suggest a little less formality, but she didn't quite have the nerve. She found Miss Kelvington's professional demeanor vaguely intimidating, as she suspected she was supposed to. So she settled for giving the nanny what she hoped was a self-assured smile and then left.

She had almost finished unpacking when the antique French phone on her bedside table began to ring. Startled, Eleanore stared at it, wondering if she should answer. It couldn't be for her. No one knew she was here except Murad and he'd hardly interrupt his date with Sonia to call her.

Ignoring the phone, she turned back to her suitcase. A few minutes later, there was a soft knock at her door and she opened it, assuming it was Miss Kelvington with Lacey. It wasn't. It was Ali.

She smiled at him. "Yes?" There was no answering smile.

"You didn't answer your ring," he accused.

"My ring? You mean that phone call? I assumed it was for someone else."

"Then your phone wouldn't have rung. All incoming calls are answered at the central switchboard and then transferred to the proper person."

"Of course," Eleanore said wryly. "I should have realized. Sorry to make you climb the stairs. Who was it?"

"Selim al-Rashid and he's still on the line. Simply—"

"No," she flatly refused, deeply resenting the fact that Murad had reported her arrival to her father.

"No?" Ali blinked in astonishment. "Selim al-Rashid is our country's oil minister. One does not refuse to speak to him."

For "one," read a female, Eleanore thought cynically. "Sorry, but I don't feel worthy of the honor." She gave Ali a bright, insincere smile.

From the look on Ali's face it was clear he agreed with her opinion, but Eleanore didn't care. She had no intention of being manipulated into speaking to her father before she was ready. She'd agreed to meet him and she would, but at a time and place of her choosing. And it most definitely wouldn't be when she was tired and rushed.

"But what am I to tell the Minister?" Ali persisted.

"The truth? Failing that, try a polite lie."

"Why don't you tell him?" Ali suggested with a crafty look that made Eleanore want to giggle. Whatever other talents Ali had, intrigue wasn't one of them. Neither, it appeared, was he aware of her relationship to Selim. The realization that Murad hadn't discussed her personal life with his secretary made her feel slightly better.

"I never talk to strange men. And besides," she added at Ali's incredulous look. "I have to hurry if I'm going to make it to the Y on time."

"You're going out?" Ali looked shocked.

"Certainly." She was a little surprised at his reaction. Surely they didn't still practice purdah in Abar?

"But His Excellency didn't mention it."

"Probably because His Excellency didn't know," she said tartly. "Not that he would have cared if he had. I'm a guest in this house, Ali. Not a prisoner."

"Yes, and as a guest every precaution must be taken for your safety. Unfortunately, Wilkerson took the staff car earlier, the Jaguar is being serviced and, of course, His Excellency is using the Rolls."

"Of course," Eleanore said. "Tell you what, my friend, you may call a cab for me when I'm ready to leave." She decided to splurge a little. Without housing expenses, her savings would last quite a while.

"A cab!" Ali repeated in tones of deepest horror.

"You ought to approve. You're the one hung up on cars."

"You wouldn't consider postponing..." He broke off as she shook her head.

"Don't fret. I'll be fine. Modern women can take care of themselves."

"In New York City? Oh, very well." Ali capitulated in the face of her implacable expression. "But His Excellency isn't going to like this."

"So don't tell him."

"Lie?" Ali looked horrified.

"There's a big difference between lying and failing to volunteer something. Now if there's nothing else I may do for you?"

"You haven't done anything for me yet," he grumbled. "You won't talk to the oil minister and you will leave the house in a . . . cab." He spat out the word.

Poor Ali, Eleanore thought as he stomped down the stairs. She felt badly that she'd upset him, but not so badly that she'd allow herself to be maneuvered into doing something she didn't want to do.

4

ELEANORE GOT TO HER FEET and made her way to the front as the bus approached the Sutton Place stop. To her dismay, the scruffy-looking young man who'd been eyeing her ever since he'd gotten on twelve blocks back was moving to the rear exit. For a second, she considered saying something to the bus driver but two things stopped her. First of all, what could she actually say? That a man was looking at her? So what? Men had been looking at women since time immemorial. It didn't necessarily mean anything. It was just that in this case, his scrutiny set off alarm bells deep within her.

Eleanore tried to convince herself that she was probably letting her imagination run away with her. More than likely the young man was simply an incipient lecher who didn't have the experience yet to disguise the fact.

And, besides—she studied the bored-looking driver as he brought the bus to a halt—she doubted he'd be much help. He had Uninvolved Bystander stamped all over him.

"Well, lady, you getting off or aren't you? I got a schedule to keep, you know," the driver snapped.

Making up her mind, Eleanore got off. She'd been riding the bus home after her nighttime tutoring sessions for almost two years now and nothing had ever happened. And her old neighborhood couldn't begin to compare with the moneyed elegance of Murad's. Besides, she reminded herself, she was a graduate of the Y's self-defense class. As a matter of fact, she'd been their best student. The thought helped to restore her normal self-confidence.

She stole a quick glance over her shoulder at the seedy young man. To her relief, he'd moved down the street and was standing in a doorway, apparently checking the number on the mailbox.

Feeling foolish, Eleanore started toward Murad's house. She was only six doors away when she heard the ominous thud of pounding feet. Bracing herself, she turned to find the man bearing down on her. Frantically, she tried to remember what to do, but her mind couldn't seem to get beyond the mask of hate that had twisted her assailant's face into something barely human.

As he reached her, one of his hands grabbed for her purse and the other hit her across the face. A gush of warm, salty blood spurted from her nose, but Eleanore refused to relinquish her death grip on her purse. It was hers, dammit! She wasn't going to calmly hand it over to some thug. She kicked out at him, managing to land a solid blow on his shin.

His grunt of angry pain sounded obscene in the darkness. She ducked as he swung a fist at her head, still refusing to give him her purse.

To her surprise, her assailant was suddenly wrenched away from her and a lean, dark figure reduced him to a crumpled heap on the pavement with a few well aimed blows.

Instinctively, she turned to escape only to be stopped by the sound of her rescuer's furious voice.

"What the hell are you doing wandering the streets of New York City at this hour?" Murad yelled.

"I'm not wandering." She took exception to the way he phrased his question. "Wandering implies no destination and I have one."

"The hospital no doubt! Stand still." He tipped her head back and tried to assess the damage to her face in the dim glow from the streetlight. "You're bleeding like a stuck pig."

His comment struck her as hilariously funny and she began to giggle. "What a poetic turn of phrase you have. I'll bet you're a real hit with the women."

Ignoring her, Murad reached into his pocket for a crisp white linen handkerchief, which he pressed against the bridge of her nose.

"Are you all right, Excellency?" the man with Murad spoke.

"Yes, Hamid," Murad said shortly. "Check the slimeball."

"You really should not have hit him, Excellency. You might have hurt your hands." Hamid grasped the back of Eleanore's assailant's sweatshirt and hauled him to his feet as if he weighed no more than Lacey.

"He hurt me." The young man sounded shocked. "I think one of my ribs is busted."

"Silence, vermin." Hamid shook him and the young man gasped in pain.

"You haven't irrevocably damaged him, Excellency." Hamid sounded regretful.

"Good thing, too," Eleanore mumbled around the handkerchief. "Bodies are the very devil to dispose of."

"Not when you have diplomatic immunity." Hamid eyed the cowering mugger speculatively.

"Hold it!" the young man yelped. "I'm an American citizen. You better not try nuthin'."

"Excellency, should I dispose of the vermin?"

"Tempting as the thought is, I think this time we'll simply turn him over to the police. File a formal complaint, but keep my birdbrained houseguest's name out of it."

"It is not her fault, Excellency." Hamid gave her a sympathetic glance. "She is only a woman."

"Yeah, it's not my fault." Eleanore began to giggle again. Maybe there were some advantages to a male-dominated society after all.

"Shock," Murad said shortly. "I'll get her home. And you, spawn of Lucifer—" his hard voice sliced frighteningly through the night "—if I ever see you again anywhere near this neighborhood..."

"You won't. There was nuthin' personal about tryin' to snatch her purse. I mean, anybody's would'a done. I'm sorry," he wailed as Hamid dragged him toward the Rolls.

"Come on." Murad put an arm around Eleanore's shoulders and gently steered her up the steps to his front door.

"It was a lucky coincidence you were coming home when you were," she said.

Coincidence had had nothing to do with it, Murad thought grimly. During the intermission of the monumentally boring play that Sonia had wanted to see, he'd slipped out and called Ali to check on how Eleanore was adjusting to his household. When Ali had told him that she'd not only gone out, but was using public transportation, he'd felt a tremendous surge of fear.

He'd called the number at the Y that Ali had given him, only to be told that Eleanore had just left to catch the bus.

Not even bothering to offer Sonia an explanation, he'd bundled her into a taxi and then tried to intercept Eleanore.

No, coincidence had had nothing to do with his arriving in time to rescue her. Not that he had any intention of telling Eleanore that. He didn't begin to understand his own compulsion to protect her. Who knew what she might make of it?

"Your Highness!" Ali swung the door wide open. "What has happened?"

"Miss Fulton's just discovered the dangers of walking the streets of New York City at night. Call Dr. Whren and tell him to come over."

"No," Eleanore objected, ignoring Ali's incredulous reaction to the idea that she would dare to countermand one of Murad's orders. "It's nothing. Really." She turned to Murad. "Once I wash the gore off, I'll be fine."

Murad studied her bloodied features with a critical eye. "Go and wash and then I'll decide whether or not to call the doctor," he finally said.

"Then *I'll* decide," Eleanore muttered, keeping her objection mild. All things considered, this wasn't the best time to complain about his tendency to take charge.

"There's a washroom in there." Murad nodded toward a door she hadn't noticed under the staircase. "When you're done, I'll be in my study."

"All right." Eleanore agreed even though she had no stomach for the coming interview. Her impulse was to escape to her room, but she knew she was going to have to face him sooner or later and listen to a lecture on her irresponsible behavior. She might as well get it over with.

Eleanore made short work of cleaning up. As she'd thought, except for a bruise on her cheekbone, where the thug's ring had caught her, there wasn't any visible damage. Opening the washroom door, she found Ali patiently waiting in the hallway.

"Are you all right, Miss Fulton?" He studied her darkening bruise.

"I'm fine. I should have listened to you and waited for a driver," she said, hoping to soothe the agitated old man. "Where's His Excellency's study?"

"This way." Ali led her down the hall and ushered her through an open door.

"Miss Fulton, Your Excellency," he announced and then quietly closed the door behind her.

Murad was sitting on the edge of a huge mahogany desk, listening to someone on the phone. He gestured Eleanore toward the brown leather chair beside him.

Eleanore sank down into it, her eyes instinctively following the hypnotic movement of his foot as it swung back and forth. She watched the subdued light from the desk lamp as it glinted off the highly polished leather of his handmade shoes. Slowly, her gaze traveled upward over his well-formed calf, past his knee, to linger on his heavily muscled thigh.

A slight flush warmed her cheeks as she began to imagine his body without the concealment of clothing. His leg would undoubtedly be as tanned as the back of his hand, which was impatiently drumming its fingers on the desktop. Eleanore's lips parted slightly, her breathing whistling unevenly through them. She could almost feel the satiny smoothness of his skin and the ripple of muscle beneath it.

"It was unavoidable, Sonia." Murad's urbane voice jarred her out of her daydream, and she shifted restlessly.

Murad shot a quick, assessing glance at her and brought his conversation to a halt. "Of course you may buy the necklace. A lovely neck like yours deserves a lovely ornament. I'll call Cartier's in the morning and authorize it. Yes, Sonia. Goodbye." He hung up and turned to Eleanore.

"Hold still a minute." Murad grasped her chin and tilted her head back while he studied her face. His harsh expletive belied his gentle fingertips as he traced over the darkening bruise on her cheek.

"It's nothing." The spicy fragrance of his cologne and the heat from his body were swamping her senses, making it exceedingly difficult for her to concentrate. She leaned back, her pride demanding that she not let him see how his casual touch was affecting her. "Really, I'm fine."

"Sure you are," he scoffed. "Look at you. You're trembling. Here, drink this." He handed her a crystal tumbler full of what looked like milk.

Grateful that he'd misinterpreted the cause of her agitation, she automatically accepted the glass. The heat from the liquid seeped into her fingers.

"Drink it," he ordered. "Then we'll talk."

Eleanore loathed warm milk, but she decided not to waste energy arguing. All she wanted to do was to get the lecture over with and escape to bed. The day's events had left her emotionally and physically drained.

She took a sip and then peered suspiciously into the glass. "It tastes strange. Did you put brandy in this?"

"Hardly," Murad said. "This is a Muslim household. If you want to drink, you'll have to indulge the urge elsewhere."

"I don't want to drink. I just...oh, never mind." She took a deep breath and drained the glass. It was probably goat's milk. Or camel's. Did one milk camels? she wondered irrelevantly.

Murad took the tumbler from her, set it on the desk behind him, and turned back to Eleanore. She shivered slightly at the implacable expression on his lean face. Reminding herself that she wasn't one of his minions, she stared back.

"I'm waiting," he said.

"For what?" she stalled.

"For an explanation of why you were being mugged."

"You heard him." Eleanore shrugged. "I was simply in the wrong spot at the wrong time. It happens a lot in New York City."

"Not to the people I'm responsible for," Murad bit out. "I left you safe at home and came back to find you being assaulted."

"I'm not a possession. I move on my own."

"Not very intelligently! Did you even think about what might happen if you used a bus late at night?"

"If I allowed myself to dwell on it, I'd become a hermit after sundown," she said. "Besides, I took lessons in self-defense."

"Then why didn't you use them?"

"It all happened so fast." She grimaced. "I mean... Well, in class you knew they were coming and..."

"That they wouldn't really hurt you?"

"Something like that," she admitted sheepishly.

"And what were you doing that couldn't have waited until a driver had been arranged?"

Eleanore opened her mouth to tell him in no uncertain terms that it was none of his business when a huge yawn almost dislocated her jaw. By the time she'd finished, she'd decided that it might be wiser to try a conciliatory approach.

"This is Wednesday—" she began.

"You always court disaster on Wednesdays?"

Eleanore's temper began to fray around the edges. Murad exasperated her more than any man she'd ever met.

"I'm a literacy volunteer and Wednesday is my regular night to tutor," she said forcing a reasonable tone.

"Not after what happened tonight," he said flatly.

"Especially after what happened tonight," Eleanore argued, knowing there was a lot more at stake here than whether or not she gave up her tutoring. Murad was highly autocratic and she suspected that if she allowed him to, he'd very quickly take over her life. The fact that he felt he was doing it for her own good was irrelevant. She'd fought too long and too hard for her independence to give it up now. Even temporarily.

"Being mugged is like falling off a horse," she said. "You have to get right back on. If I start hiding out after dark because of what happened, I'll be letting the mugger dictate how I live my life." She blinked as Murad's face wavered ever so slightly.

"There's a certain perverted logic in what you're saying," he admitted. "Suppose we compromise. You continue your nighttime tutoring, but instead of using public transportation, let someone from the household drive you back and forth."

Eleanore rubbed her forehead, trying to think. It took a considerable effort. A thick fog seemed to be encroaching on her mind, hampering her thought processes considerably. Confused, she focused on a small piece of turquoise pottery on the shelf to the right of Murad's head and forced herself to rationally weigh his offer. Her first instinct was to tell him no, and that she'd get to and from the Y by herself as she'd always done. But the more she considered his compromise, the more she realized that he was in essence offering her another type of independence. Freedom from the pervasive fear of being mugged. It would be an incredible luxury to feel really safe. And he had backed off from his initial demand that she give up her tutoring altogether, she reminded herself.

Eleanore opened her mouth to agree and was immediately consumed by another outsize yawn. "Sorry, I don't know why I'm so tired all of a sudden." She blinked, having trouble keeping her eyes open. "I'll accept a ride to my tutoring. In fact, I'd appreciate it. Now, if there's nothing else?"

"Yes."

"Yes?" she parroted in confusion.

"Yes, there's something else. I understand that your father called before you left and you refused to speak to him."

Eleanore blinked owlishly at him.

"Well?" he demanded.

"Well what? You've stated the facts. What do you want? An editorial comment?"

Murad's expression hardened at her flip tone. "What I want is an explanation."

"And if I thought you were entitled to one, I'd offer it," she shot back. "Two things, however, stop me. I dislike being spied on, and giving you information would be rewarding you for a gross invasion of privacy."

"A gross invasion of privacy! Oh, come now."

"A gross invasion of privacy," she insisted. "This is the United States. We have laws here."

"Not in this house," Murad said silkily. "This house is registered to the Abarian Consulate, The United States has no jurisdiction here."

"Pity," she slurred the word and then frowned. "Are you sure there wasn't any brandy in that milk?"

"Cross my heart," Murad said solemnly.

Eleanore watched in fascination as his long fingers moved over the darkness of his dinner jacket. She tore her gaze away and demanded, "Then why am I having trouble concentrating?"

"The sedative is probably starting to work."

"What!" Eleanore yelped, a burst of anger momentarily clearing her mind. "How dare you drug me!"

"Because without it, you'd undoubtedly have spent the night worrying about what happened."

"Of all the high-handed, overbearing—"

"You forgot concerned," Murad said mildly.

"Yes, well . . ." she sputtered to a stop, filled with a confusing mixture of emotions. To think that just a few weeks ago she'd actually wished she could sit back and let someone else take care of everything. It had seemed a very tempting idea at the time, but she was fast coming to realize that in practice it left a lot to be desired.

Nevertheless, his concern, high-handed though it was, was strangely seductive. For the first time in her life, someone seemed to realize that she might need a little help in coping with things.

"Have you gone to sleep yet?" Murad inquired politely.

"No."

"Then tell me why you refused to talk to your father. You agreed you would."

"I agreed I'd see him. A phone call is not seeing." She enunciated each word very clearly.

"You're quibbling, dammit." Murad ran his long fingers through his black hair, creating an endearingly disheveled look.

"Precision is the basis of all language," she offered.

"Eleanore!"

"All right," she shrugged. "I didn't speak to him because I didn't want to. Satisfied?"

"No, you agreed to talk to him."

"And I will, but I'll choose the place and it certainly won't be the second I set foot in your house. And another thing, I resent your telling him I was here."

"Why?"

"Because . . ." She frowned, trying to present her anger in a way that didn't make her sound like a petulant child. She couldn't. The sedative had confused her too much. "I want to go to bed," she finally said.

Murad sighed. "That's probably not a bad idea. We'll talk about this—" He broke off as the phone on his desk rang. Picking it up, he listened for a moment and then answered in what Eleanore assumed to be Arabic.

She leaned her head back against the leather chair and closed her eyes, allowing the melodic sound of

Murad's voice to flow soothingly through her mind, sending her to sleep.

She awoke to a sensation of movement. Forcing her eyelids open, she found her vision limited to a black field. A scratchy, black field. She snuggled her cheek into it. A dull thumping sound filled her ears and she struggled to identify it. It was a heartbeat. And the scratchy blackness was Murad's dinner jacket. He was carrying her somewhere.

"Where are we going?" she asked without a great deal of interest. She was much more interested in the feel of his steely arms as he effortlessly carried her high against his chest. She felt safe, truly safe for the first time in her life. A feeling she was quick to blame on her muddled thought processes.

"To bed."

"Sonia won't like that," she murmured. A vivid image of Murad bending over her, his face taut with passion, burst into her mind, and she flushed.

"Sonia has nothing to do with you."

"I'll say. She gets diamonds. I get yelled at." Her sense of injustice colored her words.

"And here I thought we were having a meaningful dialogue." Murad chuckled.

"You don't have meaningful dialogues," she grumbled. "You have confrontations." She clutched the lapel of his dinner jacket as he turned sideways to enter her bedroom.

"Poor Eleanore." His voice was threaded with laughter. "Do you want some diamonds, too? What is your American saying? Diamonds are a girl's best friend?"

"The modern version of that is that an education is a girl's best friend," she said, then squeaked as he dropped her onto her soft bed and pulled the comforter over her body.

"Go to sleep," he ordered.

The sedative dampened her normal inhibitions, and she found herself saying, "Without a good-night kiss?"

"Is that part of the treatment?" His voice deepened perceptibly as he placed a hand on the bed on either side of her head.

Eleanore peered up at him, trying to read his expression, but his face in the reflected light from the hallway was simply a pale blur. She felt the mattress depress as he leaned over her and lightly brushed his mouth to hers. Tingling sparks arced from his lips to hers, leaving an urgent desire for something more substantial in their wake.

"Murad?" She was totally oblivious of the pleading note in her voice. "I . . . you . . ."

Murad's firm lips cut off her incoherent plea and pleasure, unlike anything she'd ever felt, exploded in her. Her hands, trapped beneath the comforter, moved restlessly, aching to touch him. She felt as if she were sinking into a downy cloud of warm pleasure and then, suddenly, as if a light had been turned off, she was sound asleep.

THE NEXT THING she knew, a finger was brushing gently across her cheekbone. She shifted slightly and snuggled deeper into the down pillow, but the finger followed. Followed and began to lightly trace around her ear. A delightful shiver chased down her spine and Eleanore sighed softly in pleasure. She turned her head, blindly nuzzling the hand. The faint scent of pine soap clung to it, drifting into her mind and nudging her to full consciousness.

She rolled over and, opening her eyes, peered up. Straight into Murad's watchful eyes. For an infinitesimal moment she seemed to be drowning in the bottomless blackness of his eyes; then her memory returned and an echo of her demanding a good-night kiss filled her mind. She closed her eyes in embarrassment.

"Don't go back to sleep."

To her hypersensitive ears, his voice sounded indulgent. There appeared to be no trace of either amusement or disgust at what had happened. But then, she reasoned, what *had* happened, when all was said and done? She'd asked a man to kiss her; it was hardly worth a comment in this day and age.

Gathering her courage, she opened one eye and peered up at him. If it had been any other man, she could have made a joke of it, but what Murad did to her emotions was no joking matter.

"Come on, woman. You're halfway there. Open the other eye."

His chuckle sent a warm glow of pleasure through her. Deciding that her aunt's maxim of "least said, soonest mended" definitely applied here, she focused on the present, not the past.

"What do you want?" she asked.

"I have to leave for the office now and I wanted to tell you about tonight before I left."

"Tonight?" She sat up, grimacing at her crumpled clothing. "What about tonight?"

"I invited everyone in the office to a cocktail party here."

"You invited your entire office here? Tonight? And you're just telling me?" Her eyes glazed over in horror. "How many people is that?"

"Twenty-one including the clerks, and I'm sure most of them will be bringing husbands, wives or significant others."

"I hope one of them brings the coroner for when I murder you!" She flung off the comforter and jumped to her feet, swaying slightly as dizziness washed over her.

Murad grabbed her arm and pulled her up against him, cradling her body against his solid chest. "Take it easy until the effects of the sedative wear off." He gently rubbed her back.

"And how long is that going to take?" Her body instinctively relaxed against his, her soft curves fitting into his hard frame . . . hard, muscular frame. She frowned, remembering how he'd carried her up a flight of stairs last night. He was in surprisingly good physical shape for a supposedly decadent man.

"Not long, providing you eat your breakfast." He dipped his head and dropped a quick kiss on the soft skin behind her ear. A shower of sparks exploded in her mind, dissolving her disquieting thoughts.

"Why did you do that?" She studied his features, wondering if he felt even a fraction of the attraction that she did.

"To help you wake up." His smile was a masterpiece of innocence, but his eyes gleamed with wicked laughter.

She reluctantly concluded that Murad wasn't motivated by sexual curiosity, but by sheer devilment. And it was hardly any wonder, she thought stifling a sigh. She must look like something the cat dragged in.

"Don't worry. That bombshell about the party was more than enough to do the job," she said tartly.

"I don't see what all the fuss is about."

"All the fuss..." she sputtered. "Do you have any idea what's involved in entertaining that many people? There's making sure everything's clean."

"Wilkerson will see to that."

"And the menu."

"Gaston's province. Don't worry about a thing," he said soothingly. "The staff will take care of all the details. All you have to do is appear at the right moment to greet the guests."

"How formal is this affair?"

"I hadn't thought about it, but I guess the usual. Black tie."

"I think you're making a mistake," she warned. "I'll give you odds that ninety-nine percent of the men in your office don't own a tux."

"You think not?" Murad frowned.

"I could be wrong, but I doubt it. You'd do better to let it be known at work today that suits and cocktail dresses will be the norm. After all, the whole purpose of this affair is to get to know your staff. Driving home the differences in your respective life-styles is not going to help."

"True." Murad looked thoughtful. "Thank you for the insight." He nodded toward her bedside table. "There's a credit card and a checkbook. You'll need to buy some clothes for entertaining. Leave the receipts with Ali. You did say you had sufficient funds for your own needs, didn't you?"

"Yes," she said shortly.

"Then you're all set." He pushed back his gleaming white cuff and checked the time. "I've got to go. If you need anything, ask Ali or Wilkerson."

Eleanore was filled with a confusing mixture of emotions as she watched him leave. She hated the idea of his buying her dresses, hated anything that emphasized the disparities in their life-styles. But he was right, she would never have bought them under normal circumstances. And he wasn't throwing his money at her. He'd respected her desire to pay her personal expenses herself.

She told herself to think of the dress as a uniform. A uniform she was going to have to acquire before tonight. And shopping was going to take time, she suddenly realized. Time that she'd planned on using to try to pick up a lead on her cousin's whereabouts. She glanced at her watch.

If she hurried, she could still accomplish both things this morning after she'd given Lacey her bottle.

5

"DON'T GO TO SLEEP YET, angel." Eleanore wiggled the nipple of the bottle in Lacey's mouth in an attempt to get her to finish the last bit of formula. It was futile. Lacey gave her a milky smile, a tremendous burp, and then her eyelids firmly closed.

"Don't worry about the last half ounce." Miss Kelvington deftly scooped the baby out of Eleanore's arms and gently laid her on her stomach in the crib. "A baby knows when it's had enough, and she's certainly healthy." She pulled the fluffy blanket up around Lacey's tiny ears.

"At the moment." Eleanore sighed. "Lacey just got over what seemed like her tenth bout of upper respiratory infection."

"She'll do much better now that I'm in charge of her care," Miss Kelvington said complacently, and Eleanore couldn't decide whether to be insulted or amused by the woman's presumption. The gentle pat she placed on Lacey's humped bottom tipped the balance to amusement. Miss Kelvington might be an arrogant egomaniac about her own capabilities, but she clearly loved children.

"I'm going to be out this morning, but I'll take care of Lacey this afternoon," Eleanore said. "And this evening there's a dinner party."

"Yes, I know. His Excellency mentioned it when he was here earlier."

"Murad was here? In the nursery?" Eleanore asked in disbelief.

"To say good morning to Lacey. He's very good with her, too. He holds her just as he ought to. She looks somewhat like him around the eyes," Miss Kelvington offered with seeming casualness.

"What?" Eleanore blinked.

"Little Lacey. I said she looks something like His Excellency around the eyes," Miss Kelvington repeated, her own eyes seething with rampant curiosity.

"Lacey looks just like my cousin." Eleanore gave the woman a nod and hastily escaped, appalled by the woman's insinuations. Had the rest of the household drawn the same conclusions as Miss Kelvington? And what about the people from his office that she'd be meeting tonight? Would they think she was a former lover who'd suddenly erupted back into his life carrying an embarrassing reminder of the past?

Sighing, Eleanore started down the stairs, telling herself that she should have realized that this might happen. Simply because Murad had told everyone that Lacey was her niece and she, herself, was a friend of the family, that didn't mean people would believe him.

She paused on the second-floor landing as another aspect of the situation occurred to her. Did Murad know what Miss Kelvington thought? Before last night she'd have thought he wasn't perceptive enough to realize what the nanny suspected. But that incident with the mugger had shown her a totally unexpected facet of his personality, as if for a brief second a door had opened up and she'd caught a glimpse of an entirely different man.

"Ah, there you are, madam."

Eleanore turned in the direction of a very English-sounding voice and found herself confronting what had to be the epitome of the proper English butler. Talk about conspicuous consumption, she thought, biting back a nervous giggle. She felt as if she'd fallen behind the looking glass. All it needed was the Mad Hatter. Or, perhaps, the Queen of Hearts, she thought, remembering Murad's reference to his father.

"Yes, Mr. . . ."

"Wilkerson, madam. I am the butler."

"I'm pleased to meet you, Mr. Wilkerson. Murad mentioned you last night."

"No, madam. Simply Wilkerson," he corrected her.

"All right, simply Wilkerson. Did you want me?"

"The phone in your room was ringing while you were up in the nursery."

"It doesn't matter." Eleanore shrugged. "I haven't given this number to anyone."

"No, it wasn't the house phone that was ringing, madam. It was the one on your desk. Its number is the one you had in your apartment."

"It is? How'd you do that?"

"It's just call forwarding, madam. At any rate, someone was trying to reach you a few minutes ago."

"Why didn't you answer it?" Eleanore demanded in frustration. It could have been Kelly finally calling.

"His Excellency gave express orders that no one but you was to answer that phone."

"I see," Eleanore said, realizing Murad was right. Her aunt would panic if strange men started answering when she called what she thought was her niece's apartment. And there certainly were some strange men in this household, Eleanore thought ruefully.

"If you wish, I can easily hook up an answering machine to the phone. Then you won't miss any more calls."

"Thank you, Wilkerson." She gave him a grateful smile. "That's a good idea."

"Yes, it is, but I can't take credit for it. His Excellency suggested it before he left. Very thorough, he is."

"Is he?" Very thorough didn't sound like the Murad Ahiqar who had been featured on the cover of every scandal sheet in town. But it did describe the Murad Ahiqar who had calmly dispatched her assailant last night.

"What would madam like for breakfast?"

"Coffee and not to be called madam. It makes me feel like something out of a bordello."

"A bordello!" Wilkerson looked shocked to the depths of his English soul.

"A bordello," she repeated. "I prefer Eleanore. If you prefer something more formal, use Miss Fulton."

"Could we compromise with Miss Eleanore?" He looked uncertain.

"Done," she agreed, even though she wasn't certain it was an improvement. Miss Eleanore made her feel like a character from *Gone with the Wind*. "I'll be down for my coffee as soon as I've made a call. Say five minutes?"

Wilkerson nodded majestically. "At your convenience, Miss Eleanore."

Hurrying into her bedroom, she quickly located the phone Wilkerson had mentioned. It was sitting on an exquisite marquetry desk.

Who could have called? It wouldn't have been the school. She'd already told her principal she'd be un-available for substitute teaching for the next few months. Maybe it had been her aunt?

There was an easy way to find out. Eleanore reached for the phone and dialed her number.

It was immediately apparent that her earlier caller had indeed been her aunt. It was also clear that her aunt still didn't know that Kelly had disappeared; her sole topic of conversation was her husband's latest drunken binge.

"That's too bad," Eleanore murmured patiently, having long ago learned that her aunt didn't want con-structive advice. She wanted sympathy, sympathy that Eleanore lavished on her from the depths of her own love. Eleanore might feel that her aunt was foolish to stay with a man who, even during his infrequent bouts of sobriety, had little to recommend him, but she kept that opinion strictly to herself.

"Aunt Theresa, do you remember Barbra Majoric?" she interjected when her aunt paused for breath.

"Barbra Majoric?" Her aunt had trouble shifting topics.

"Kelly's best friend her first three years of high school. Her family moved to Ohio between her junior and senior year. She told Kelly she'd be returning to New York City for college. Do you know if she did?"

"Oh, her." Theresa sounded less than enthusiastic. "I never could like that child, no matter how hard I tried. She never really looks at you, if you know what I mean."

"Uh-huh." Eleanore shared her aunt's reservations about Barbra. She'd always felt the girl was a bad influence on the impressionable Kelly. "But do you know if she's back in the city?"

"Yes. As a matter of fact her mother dropped me a line a few weeks ago and asked me to keep an eye on her. Although what she thinks I could do when her own parents have absolutely no control over her—"

"Could I have her address, Aunt Theresa?"

"Just a minute, dear. I wrote it in my book here. Have you got a pencil handy?"

"Yes." Eleanore grabbed the gold pen sitting beside the notepad and scribbled down the address. "Thanks a lot, Aunt Theresa. I appreciate it."

"Glad to help, dear, although I can't imagine what you want with Barbra. Will you and Kelly be able to bring Lacey to visit this weekend? I'd love to see you all." Theresa sounded wistful.

"Kelly's probably going to be pretty busy this weekend getting ready for the start of classes." Eleanore prayed her words were true. "Why don't we give her a few weeks to get into the routine of studying before we all come home. Although I could bring Lacey out for a few hours next Wednesday. I'm free that day."

"Thank you, dear." Theresa sighed. "You're such a comfort to me. Thank heavens your mother never cared for responsibility or I wouldn't have had the pleasure of raising you."

"Bye, Aunt Theresa. See you next week." Eleanore slowly hung up the phone, her mind on her aunt's unexpected words. Never cared for responsibility. Theresa had never said anything like that before. Or maybe she had and she'd simply ignored what she didn't want to hear. Or maybe Murad's accusations about her mother's duplicity had made her more critical? The idea bothered her, but she knew this wasn't the time to try to sort it out. She had far too much to do this morning.

Grabbing her purse, she stuffed the credit card and checkbook Murad had given her into it and headed downstairs for her coffee. First, she intended to visit Barbra and ask if she knew where Kelly was, and then she would see about finding herself a couple of dressy outfits. It was going to be awkward enough playing hostess to a bunch of people she'd never met without being inappropriately dressed.

She refused Ali's offer of a car and driver because of a nagging fear that the driver would automatically report her movements to Murad. And, while she didn't think he'd wonder about her visit to Barbra, the foresight he'd shown in having her apartment phone number forwarded bothered her. Especially when added to his decisive behavior last night when he'd rescued her from the mugger. She was probably being overly cautious, but on the off chance that she wasn't, she'd play it safe and not give Murad any clues to the fact that Lacey wasn't her daughter. She simply didn't know him well enough to predict how he'd react. It was entirely possible that he might refuse to put up with the inconvenience of Lacey and her nanny.

It was not a risk she was prepared to take. Not when there was no need for it. She'd be safe enough on public transportation in broad daylight.

Finding Barbra's apartment proved relatively simple. It was in a rather run-down building on the edge of Columbia University's campus.

Eleanore double-checked the name on the door and then rang the bell.

A few seconds later the door was flung open to reveal Barbra dressed in a crumpled shirt and dirty jeans. Had everyone slept in their clothes last night? Eleanore wondered with a flash of amusement.

"Do you know what time it is?" Barbra demanded belligerently.

"Time for you to grow up." Eleanore wrinkled her nose at the unmistakable odor of marijuana clinging to the girl.

"Mind your own business," Barbra snapped. "What do you want?"

"Kelly."

"What? Has poor old Kel escaped? Good for her."

"Maybe, but it's not so good for Lacey."

"So?" Barbra shrugged. "What's it got to do with me? As you can see, I didn't do a flit with her. So beat it."

"Has she been in touch with you?" Eleanore persisted.

"No, she hasn't been in touch with me," Barbra mimicked. "And if she had, I wouldn't tell *you*. Now get lost!" Barbra slammed the door in Eleanore's face.

Eleanore suppressed an impulse to bang on the door, knowing that she wouldn't get any more information today. Not because of any sense of loyalty on Barbra's part to Kelly, but more from a desire to thwart Eleanore.

Eleanore turned and made her way out of the building. She'd wait a couple of days and then try again. But for now, she'd do better to concentrate on buying the dresses she needed. The thought of her shopping expedition sent a flash of pleasure through her. Shopping when she didn't have to check the price tag first was going to be a new experience for her. It also turned out to be a very productive one.

THAT EVENING before the party Eleanore smiled in satisfaction as she studied the four cocktail dresses hanging in her closet. Not only were they appropriate for entertaining, but they were also exceedingly becoming. Any of the four would turn her into a jet-set hostess. At least outwardly. She tried to ignore the shiver of apprehension that skittered through her.

Deciding to wear the deep garnet-red gown for the evening's party, Eleanore removed it from its protective plastic bag and slipped it over her head, sighing in pleasure as its cool silkiness slithered over her skin. She fastened the two large buttons at the waist that held the dress together and studied herself in the mirror. She still had doubts about the ability of the crossover bodice to stay crossed over despite the saleslady's earnest assurances. She'd feel a lot more secure if she had a safety pin to anchor it with, she thought, and then grimaced at her reflection in the mirror.

"You, my girl, have the sophistication of a potato. This dress is all the fashion and nothing's going to happen." At least nothing was going to happen provided she remembered not to make any sudden movements.

Reaching for her makeup kit, Eleanore began to smooth on moisturizer as she considered the evening ahead.

Murad had said he'd invited everyone in the office, from the clerical staff to the two directors. She wondered how they felt about being superseded by Murad, who appeared to have no qualifications for the position other than his last name.

Unfortunately for them, family businesses tended to be run by family members, even if they needed a lot of help to do it. And Murad certainly would. His idea of an investment that paid dividends was no doubt buying jewelry for Sonia. Ah, well, the feelings of the company's co-directors was none of her business.

Carefully, she tugged a comb through her thick mass of curls. Her responsibilities were limited to playing hostess. A nervous spasm hit her stomach at the thought. It was not a role that she particularly relished. While she thoroughly enjoyed talking to individuals, she found the thought of being responsible for several dozen at a time vaguely daunting. But the principles of putting people at ease were the same, she told herself. People were people.

An image of Murad's features floated through her mind: his dark eyes glistening with humor, his ebony hair slightly disheveled as if he'd run his long fingers through it and his lips lifted in a wicked smile. No, she amended, people were not people. Some had been given a disproportionate share of gifts by a seemingly capricious fate.

A brisk knock on her bedroom door broke into her reverie, and she hurried to answer it, almost tripping in her haste. She frowned at her sandals, which were a little more than thin silver straps attached to three-inch heels. They were gorgeous to look at, but extremely treacherous to walk in.

She swung her door open, expecting to find Miss Kelvington with Lacey. It wasn't. It was Murad. A very elegant Murad wearing a light-gray three-piece suit. The pristine whiteness of his shirt provided a stark contrast to his bronze skin. The very severity of his outfit seemed to emphasize his extreme masculinity.

Eleanore took a deep breath as she felt herself being caught up in the aura of sexual magnetism he was projecting. Unconsciously projecting, she realized as she saw only curiosity in his eyes. He wasn't making an attempt to ensnare her. And why should he? Men who could attract women like Sonia Levingham didn't normally waste their time on twenty-nine-year-old schoolteachers. *Look on the bright side*, she told herself with wry humor, *at least you have novelty value*.

"Are you ill, Eleanore?" Murad pressed the back of his hand against her cheek. "You're flushed."

"Just a little nervous about this evening." She took a hasty step backward, caught her heel in the thick pile of the carpet and fell sideways.

Murad grabbed her, yanking her up against his chest. "If that's a sample of how well you walk in those—" he frowned at her sandals "—those ridiculous excuses for shoes, you're right to be nervous. You could break your neck coming down the stairs."

"Don't be silly. I can handle the shoes. It's the guests that are worrying me."

"Relax, Eleanore, they're just the people from my office. All you have to do is make soothing murmurs." His hand slipped inside the neckline of her dress and he began to gently knead the tense muscles at the base of her neck.

She barely heard his words. She was too busy concentrating on the deep vibrant tones of his husky voice and the feel of his caressing fingers. Closing her eyes, she snuggled against him. The smooth fabric of his suit jacket touched her cheek and the crisp smell of clean linen, combined with the more elusive aroma of his musky cologne, teased her nose, making her excruciatingly aware of him as a sensual being.

He moved his hand slightly, rubbing his thumb across the hollow in her throat. The movement sent a surge of warmth through her, making her breasts feel hot and full. Slowly, his hand slipped lower, his fingertips brushing against the slight swell of her breast. Eleanore trembled at the force of the desire building within her. Willing herself to concentrate on something else, she said, "Tell me about your colleagues."

"What do you want to know?" His fingers continued their insidious movement, sending tiny pinpricks of sensation into her muscles, loosening them and making her limbs go limp. The hectic flush on her cheeks deepened and seemed to engulf her entire body.

Agitatedly, Eleanore moistened her lower lip and said, "Oh, just . . . who's who and what to expect."

"Hmm . . ."

Eleanore shivered as the sound he made reverberated through his chest and was absorbed into hers.

"According to the report my father had prepared for me, it's a small office divided into three tiers of employees. The top tier consists of two directors who keep abreast of economic developments and decide where to invest. The next tier has three men and their job is to manage the investments once they're made. The bottom tier consists of administrative assistants, word processors, filing clerks, and the like."

"The ones who make the whole thing work, you mean."

Murad looked down at her. "How so?"

"Well, I don't know how businesses in the Middle East are run, but I worked part-time in a variety of offices here in New York City when I was going to college, and the vast majority of administrative assistants I've known could do their bosses' jobs with no trouble at all. In fact, sometimes they do. Quite often an executive who performs better than his peers simply has a more efficient administrative assistant."

"An executive rises on his own knowledge," Murad argued.

"Ideally, but in this country, at least, I think you'll find that office politics play an important role in promotions. And administrative assistants are in an excellent position to pass on all kinds of office gossip to their bosses."

Murad's caressing hands went still and he frowned thoughtfully into the distance, his mind clearly elsewhere.

Eleanore forced herself to move out of the haven of his arms, determined to treat their embrace as casually as he did.

She watched him, wondering what he was thinking. Her comments had hardly been revolutionary, even to someone not used to the way businesses operated. "What's the matter?" she finally asked.

"What?" He blinked and then, seeming to remember her presence, said, "Nothing. I was simply lost in admiration at the magnificence of your dress."

"Sure you were," she snapped, annoyed at his glib compliment. She wanted him to react to her as an individual, not as part of a parade of women.

"It is a magnificent dress," he insisted. "That deep red makes your skin gleam like a pearl. But it needs something." He reached out and lightly traced a finger over her skin along the edge of the bodice's deep neckline. Heat seemed to flow from his fingers, making her already sensitized breasts ache.

"I know." She concentrated on what he was saying and not on how he was making her feel. "It needs a safety pin."

"Does it fall open?" His eyes began to gleam with a teasing light that made her distinctly nervous.

"Not without help."

He grinned at her. "I'm a very helpful man."

"I can just imagine."

"Imagination is no substitute for reality."

"It doesn't take that much imagination. The scandal sheets were quite specific."

"Surely you aren't naive enough to believe everything you read in the papers?"

"I'm not naive, period. Neither am I stupid."

"Good. I think," he added ruefully. "At any rate, your dress needs something to set it off."

"Do you really think so?" She turned back to the mirror. The neckline did look a little bare. Too bare?

"Uh-huh. It needs a necklace. Something along the lines of a simple diamond pendant."

"Drat! And I went and left my jewel case at home."

"No problem. I'll lend you something."

"Thanks, but..." She was about to refuse on general principles, when he grabbed her arm and pulled her along beside him.

"Where are we going?" she asked as she cautiously descended the front stairs.

"My study."

"Your guests will be arriving momentarily, Miss Eleanore." Wilkerson's majestic voice halted them as they crossed the hall. "Would you care to inspect the buffet?"

"Not if you're satisfied, Wilkerson," Eleanore said. "You know much more about entertaining than I do."

"Thank you, Miss Eleanore." Wilkerson allowed himself an infinitesimal smile of satisfaction.

Murad pulled her into his study, closed the door and then said, "Miss Eleanore?"

"It was either that or madam." She grimaced. "I think Wilkerson is trying to be friendly."

"Wilkerson!" Murad stared at her in astonishment. "The mind boggles at the very thought."

"Is there a Mrs. Wilkerson?" Eleanore asked curiously.

"No, he'd never forget his dignity so far as to—"

"Well, don't stop now. You were just getting interesting!"

"If you're interested, I'd be only too glad to give you a firsthand demonstration." Murad's eyes gleamed with wicked laughter.

"With twenty-odd guests due any minute, we wouldn't have a cocktail party, we'd have an orgy!"

"True. We'll wait till they're gone," he teased and Eleanore felt a wave of longing engulf her. Telling herself not to be ridiculous, she watched as he turned to the picture on the wall and, moving it aside, began to open the safe behind it.

"How incredibly clichéd." Eleanore laughed. "A wall safe behind a picture."

"I'm a traditionalist. Hadn't you noticed?"

"It's hard not to notice when you persist in beating people over the head with the fact." She watched curiously as he pulled out a leather jewelry case. Opening it, he picked up a fragile silver chain, from which hung the largest diamond Eleanore had ever seen. She watched in fascination as the gem sparkled in the reflected light from the desk lamp.

She knew she shouldn't borrow it. She was already taking enough from him. But what would be the harm if the necklace spent the evening around her neck instead of in the safe? There was no way she could possibly harm a diamond, even if she'd wanted to. She looked at it longingly. Murad was right. It would set off her dress to perfection.

She made up her mind. "It's absolutely gorgeous and I'd very much like to wear it this evening."

The pleased smile on his face made her glad she'd accepted.

"Turn around," he said.

Obediently, she turned. She shivered as his warm fingers brushed across the fine hairs on the back of her neck when he fastened the chain.

He turned her toward the large antique mirror over the fireplace and studied her reflection with evident satisfaction.

"Perfect," he pronounced.

"Yes," she murmured dreamily. The old glass was slightly distorted, giving their image a dreamlike quality.

Shaking herself free of the spell, she asked, "By the way, how are we going to have a cocktail party without liquor?"

"No problem. We'll simply serve fruit punch, soda and coffee. It has its advantages. We won't have to make sure all the drunks get home safely." He tilted his dark head to one side at the sound of the doorbell. "Speaking of our guests, they appear to be arriving. Shall we greet them?"

"Might as well." Eleanore took the arm he offered and, taking a deep breath, headed for the front door.

6

ELEANORE WAS HARD-PRESSED to keep from laughing as she watched the trio of men who managed the company's investments greet Murad in unison. It was almost as if they were afraid to let one another out of sight for fear one might somehow gain an advantage.

Murad introduced them. "Eleanore, this is Mr. Todd Abrams, Mr. Jack Saunders and Mr. Paul Evans. Gentlemen, Miss Fulton."

"Just call me Todd." Abrams gave her a gleaming white smile.

Eleanore smiled noncommittally, distrustful of so much calculated charm.

When the ringing of the doorbell signaled the arrival of yet another guest, the trio gave a final social murmur and moved as one toward the refreshment table.

Eleanore caught the sudden tension in Murad's body and glanced toward the door, her spirits sinking as she caught sight of the gorgeous blonde artfully posed in the doorway.

"Miss Sonia Levingham," Wilkerson's stentorian tones sounded faintly disapproving to Eleanore's sensitive ears. It was a sentiment she heartily echoed. Why had Murad invited Sonia to what was, in essence, an office party? She certainly wasn't going to fit in with the staff. Although . . . Eleanore almost grinned at the expression on Evans's face. He was staring at Sonia as if he'd just caught sight of heaven.

Eleanore watched in unwilling admiration as the woman undulated across the reception hall toward them, her voluptuous body moving enticingly beneath the thin silk of her long, tight gown.

"Darling, you aren't mad at your little fairy, are you?" Sonia leaned up against Murad, giving him a strategic view of her more-than-ample cleavage. "I was just sure you wouldn't mind if I gate-crashed your little affair. I get so lonely without you." Her full, red lips pouted provocatively.

Eleanore watched, torn between disgust that a grown woman could act so infantile and admiration at how well she did it.

"Oh!" Sonia turned toward Eleanore with a poorly feigned start of surprise. "I didn't notice you, ma'am. I never have eyes for anyone but my Sweetums." She smiled archly. "I'll bet you don't know who I am?"

"Of course I do, you're Sonia Levingham," Eleanore displayed her most charming smile. After all, there could be no doubt Sonia was welcome, even if for some reason, Murad hadn't invited her in the first place. She stifled a sigh at the bemused expression on Murad's face. Honestly, she thought in exasperation, didn't the man have any sense? Little fairy, indeed! It was enough to make one gag. An imp of mischief grabbed her. Evans was about to meet the girl of his dreams.

"You must let me introduce you to our other guests." Eleanore took the woman's arm and pulled her toward the double living room. Sonia had no choice but to follow, leaving Murad alone to greet the next batch of arriving guests.

After having introduced Sonia to the embarrassingly enthusiastic Evans, Eleanore was immediately accosted by one of the typists she'd met earlier, a young redhead named Beth.

"Eleanore," Beth greeted her as though they were old friends. "I've been longing for a heart-to-heart chat with you."

Eleanore hastily stifled a smile at the world-weary look that sat so oddly on Beth's young face.

"Oh, dear. Was I that obvious?" Beth sighed as she noticed the twinkle in Eleanore's eye. "And I was trying so hard to sound sophisticated."

"Why?" Eleanore asked curiously.

"To show Todd that I can be a social asset," she said earnestly. "I love him so much I couldn't bear to let him down."

It was much more likely that he'd let Beth down, Eleanore thought, remembering the calculated charm in Todd Abrams's eyes, but she said nothing. For one thing, she could be wrong and, for another, even if she weren't, it was none of her business.

"You'll be fine," Eleanore reassured the younger woman. "The trick at cocktail parties is to ask a lot of questions and look fascinated by the answers."

"Not at this one." Beth grimaced. "I'd probably wind up suspected."

"Of what? Good manners?" Eleanore smiled. To her surprise, Beth didn't smile back.

"Our office oversees billions of dollars worth of investments and too much curiosity is considered bad form."

"Well, you may not be able to ask questions, but I can." Eleanore decided to get some information while she had the chance. "I've been trying to keep all these people straight, but it's hard without some kind of framework to put them in. Would you help me?"

"Sure, what do you want to know?"

"First of all, who's who?"

"Well . . ." Beth tapped her pink-polished fingernail against her front tooth. "Mr. Walton, over there by the grand piano, and Mr. Talbort run the office."

"Which one is Mr. Talbort? I don't remember meeting him." Eleanore glanced around the room.

"He isn't here. His wife has multiple sclerosis, poor thing, and she's sensitive about going out in public in a wheelchair, and he won't leave her alone at night. It's because Mr. Talbort spends so much time with her that Mr. Walton has gotten the upper hand in the office, even though they're supposed to be equals."

"I see," Eleanore said slowly.

"Then, there's Saunders and Evans and Todd. They're the administrators. And all the rest are like me, they don't really count," she said with a cheerful lack of concern. "Except for the Spider Woman . . ." A look of horror crossed Beth's face. "I can't believe I actually said that."

"Don't worry," Eleanore assured her. "I never repeat things."

"Not even to . . ." Beth looked toward Murad, whose eyes appeared glued to Sonia's cleavage.

"Especially not to him," Eleanore said tartly, thoroughly annoyed at Murad. How could he behave like an adolescent in the grip of a hormone imbalance? And do it so blatantly. As if he didn't care who saw how besotted he was.

Her gaze swung to Walton, the rotund little man by the piano who Beth said actually controlled the office. He was also watching Murad, a disdainful expression on his face.

"The Spider Woman is what we all call Ms Paulson," Beth confided, nodding toward a severely dressed woman of about forty standing by the refreshment table. "She's Mr. Walton's administrative aide and from the way she gives orders to the rest of us you'd think she was the one in charge."

"Bossy, huh?" Eleanore said sympathetically.

"She's a bitch," Beth said bluntly. "But it doesn't do any good to complain. Mr. Walton just takes her word for everything. We were all kind of hoping when we heard that His Excellency was taking over the running of the office that—" She glanced over at Murad who was listening to Sonia with rapt attention. "But I guess not...." Beth heaved a sigh.

"It's early days yet and from what he's said, he's never had much to do with business before," Eleanore temporized.

"Well, I won't have to put up with Ms Paulson much longer." Beth brightened. "Just as soon as Todd and I have enough saved for a down payment on a nice house out on the Island, we're going to get married."

"Congratulations."

"Please don't tell anyone," Beth begged. "It's supposed to be a secret. Mr. Walton doesn't like office romances."

"I wouldn't dream of saying anything," Eleanore assured her.

Just then Todd joined them. "And what are you two gorgeous women gossiping about?"

"Why, men, of course," Eleanore responded to the mute appeal in Beth's eyes. "Now, if you'll excuse me. I really must circulate." Eleanore moved away, pretending not to notice when Abrams tried to grasp her arm.

Murad seemed to materialize beside her. "What are you thinking about?"

Eleanore jumped. "Don't do that. What's the matter? Did you slip your leash?"

"I'd like to leash that tongue of yours. Haven't you ever heard you can catch more flies with honey than vinegar?"

"I'll remember that if I should ever want any flies," she shot back. "And I was thinking that it was a shame I didn't invite Liz."

"Yes." Murad chuckled. "A psychologist would have a field day with this group. Why don't we wander over and speak to Ms Paulson? She's frowning into her punch as if she's just found a bug. I don't think she approves of us."

"From what I hear, she doesn't approve of anyone," Eleanore answered absently, her mind on what Murad had said. How did he know Liz was a psychologist? He'd never met her and she was almost certain she'd hadn't mentioned her friend's profession. But if she hadn't how did Murad know? Unless Mrs. Benton had mentioned it that time she'd shared an elevator with him. That was probably it, she thought, wondering what else the woman had told him.

"Ah, Ms Paulson. I hope you are enjoying yourself." Murad gave the woman a beaming smile.

"Yes, of course. It's a lovely party," she responded politely.

"You must find your work fascinating," Eleanore said conversationally.

"Why?" Ms Paulson gave her a beady-eyed stare and Eleanore suddenly understood why the junior staff called her the Spider Woman.

"Well, the uncertainty of high finance and all that." Eleanore shrugged.

"Mr. Walton is not at all uncertain," Ms Paulson said. "He's done a marvelous job of making money for the Ahiqar family."

"And been well rewarded for his efforts," Eleanore answered as Murad appeared to lose interest in the conversation and allowed his gaze to drift longingly back to Sonia.

Annoyed, Eleanore gave him a surreptitious kick in the ankle.

Recalled, he picked up the conversational ball. "Mr. Walton has a great deal of help in making his decisions."

"Especially from Mr. Abrams," Ms Paulson said enthusiastically. "He is a very up-and-coming investment analyst, Your Excellency. Why, I wouldn't be surprised if he didn't outstrip Mr. Walton's financial acumen in the not-too-distant future."

Eleanore eyed the two dull-red patches on Ms Paulson's sallow cheeks in surprise. Was everyone in the office smitten with Abrams's practiced charms? No wonder Beth didn't like the woman. Ms Paulson must make life very hard for someone she saw as a rival for Abrams's affections.

"Who might be outstripping me?" Mr. Walton had heard his aide's comment as he joined them.

"Oh, I . . ." Ms Paulson flushed.

"Ms Paulson was simply complimenting Murad on his excellent grasp of the financial situation." Eleanore, her ready sympathy aroused, came to Ms Paulson's rescue. Sooner or later, every woman fell in love with someone she shouldn't or couldn't have. It was just too bad that the focus of Ms Paulson's passion was in the office. It could make for an awkward situation all around.

"Ah, yes, our budding financial genius." The sneer in Walton's voice was barely hidden.

Eleanore shot Murad a worried glance but he didn't seem to have heard. He was staring across the room at Sonia, who was regaling a mesmerized Mr. Saunders with what appeared to be a risqué story, judging from the faintly amused, faintly shocked expressions on the people around them.

"Excuse me," Murad murmured and headed straight for Sonia. Ms Paulson, with a furtive glance at Mr. Walton, also made her escape.

"Well, that's one thing he doesn't need any instruction in," Mr. Walton said.

"Nor in acting the autocrat," Eleanore said levelly. "A fact you'd do well to remember, Mr. Walton."

"Oh, come now, Miss... It is *Miss*, isn't it?" The sneer was pronounced.

"Perhaps you'd like to discuss my marital status with His Excellency?" Eleanore stared down her nose at the repugnant little man.

"No, no." He held his chubby fingers in front of his face. "His sexual proclivities are none of my business."

"Then refrain from making cracks about them," Eleanore snapped.

"Or what?" Mr. Walton's jovial manner disappeared.

"Or find yourself a job in an organization you can be loyal to."

"So serious at a party, Eleanore?" Murad unexpectedly rejoined them. "Don't tell me you've been lecturing her on investment strategy, Walton?"

"On the contrary, Miss Fulton has been lecturing me on the wisdom of leaving your organization."

"Eleanore!" Murad gave her a shocked look. "Don't undermine me. We'd be lost without Mr. Walton."

Why should I undermine you, Eleanore thought in exasperation, *when you're doing such a good job of it yourself.* She felt like a mother who'd just vehemently defended her child, only to have him calmly repeat the offense in front of his accusers.

"Come on. I'll get you something to drink." Murad put an arm around her shoulders and urged her toward the bar. The roughness of his suit jacket against her bare arm was sending shivers of awareness cascading down her nerve endings, where they exploded into goose bumps.

Why did she react so strongly to Murad? She worried the question around in her mind, but her mind was in no position to answer. It was a jumble of confused emotions: fury at Walton's derogatory manner to Murad; anger at Murad's failure to see it; and, most of all, annoyance at herself that she even cared.

She glanced over her shoulder at Walton, who was watching them with a satisfied smirk on his face.

"Look happy, Eleanore," Murad ordered. "That scowl on your face is beginning to worry people."

"I'd like to worry that overstuffed twit." She glared at Walton.

"What was the line from Ecclesiastes? 'For everything there is a season'?"

Eleanore frowned, wondering what he meant. Probably nothing, she finally decided, watching as Sonia, catching Murad's eye, beckoned to him.

"Behave yourself," Murad ordered and then hurried to the blonde's side.

Eleanore glanced at the antique clock on the marble mantel, wondering how much longer this affair would last. Briefly, she considered sneaking away, but her pride prevented such a cowardly course of action. She'd agreed to be Murad's hostess and hostesses didn't decamp when the going got rough. Besides, that fat little toad Walton would think he'd routed her if she left. She glanced across the room to where he was now carrying on a whispered conversation with Ms Paulson.

"Did you run afoul of the emperor?" Beth's sympathetic voice captured her attention.

"Is that what you call him?"

"That's the only repeatable thing the office calls him." Beth laughed. "Although in all fairness, he's very good at his job. It's just that when he tells you to jump, he expects you to ask 'how high?' on the way up."

"Charming."

"He can be when he gets his own way," Beth said seriously. "It's a good thing Murad is like he is or there would have been an awful fight."

"Like he is?" Eleanore asked.

"You know, more socially minded. Not interested in the business side of things."

"The Lord works in mysterious ways," Eleanore muttered. "And now, if you'll excuse me, I'd better mingle." She gave Beth a warm smile and went to rescue a young woman who appeared to be trying to hide behind a huge potted plant. She was determined to see this through to the bitter end.

The bitter end finally came almost two hours later when Wilkerson closed the door behind the last guest.

"Thank you for all the trouble you went to arranging the party, Wilkerson." Eleanore stifled a yawn. "Please convey my appreciation to the staff."

"Certainly, Miss Eleanore."

"Have you seen Murad?" She glanced around the empty hallway.

"Not recently, but I did hear Miss Levingham ask him to take her home about fifteen minutes ago." Wilkerson's button-black eyes shone with what Eleanore very much feared was sympathy. A sympathy she instantly rejected. Sonia wasn't a threat to her. Not really. Sonia had no part of Murad except his libido. And once that appeal faded, Sonia would be gone.

"Good night, Wilkerson." Eleanore turned toward the stairs and then, remembering that she was still wearing Murad's valuable necklace, headed toward the study instead. She'd leave it on his desk and he could put it back in the safe in the morning. Opening the door, she crossed the thick oriental rug, examining its complicated design as she walked. Noticing a flaw in the pattern, she bent down to examine it.

"What are you doing huddled there on the floor?" Murad's voice from behind the door startled her and she jerked around, catching her sandal's thin heel in the thick pile and falling backward.

"Honestly, Eleanore." Murad reached down and deftly hauled her to her feet, steadying her against his body.

Eleanore's mouth became dry as his hard muscles pressed against her much softer curves. She hastily took a step back, caught her heel again and stumbled.

Murad swiftly grabbed her, pulling her back up against him. "Don't move," he ordered. Bending over, he began to unbuckle her sandals. His fingers brushed against her nylon-clad feet, setting off a deep quivering in her abdomen.

"There," he said. "Now, step out of those things."

Eleanore did, hoping he'd attribute her heightened color to annoyance at his high-handed manner. "I like these shoes," she said, feeling obligated to defend them.

"I do, too . . . in the abstract. But watching you wear them is like waiting for a ticking bomb to explode." He tossed the sandals into the wastebasket beside his desk.

"You can't throw those away!"

"I not only can, I just did. Think of it as an example of 'the Lord giveth and the Lord taketh away.'" He gave her an angelic smile.

"Of all the pompous, egotistical . . ." She sputtered to an indignant stop. "If that's the way you're going to behave, you can take back everything you bought."

"Go ahead." He folded his arms across his chest and gave her a boyishly hopeful look that immediately put her on red alert.

"Go ahead what?" She eyed him suspiciously.

"You were about to fling the purchases I'd paid for back in my face, and if I'm not mistaken, that dress you're wearing was one of them. Go ahead, you have my complete attention."

"What I'm going to have is your head! I am not here for your sexual titillation—which reminds me, what happened to the vacuous blonde?"

"Nothing happened to her. At least, not at my hands," he said. "She wanted to go home so I had Ali take her. Why do you care? I assure you, Sonia is more than capable of looking out for herself."

"Yes, I know. I saw the necklace she was wearing," Eleanore said.

"There's no reason for you to be jealous. If you'll remember, I offered you a diamond necklace, too."

"I am not jealous! And I don't want one. I'd hate to get lost in the crowd."

"Believe me, there's not the slightest chance of that. You are most definitely unique," Murad said dryly. "Am I to take it that after that come-on, you aren't going to deliver?"

"I'll deliver the dress, all right, but by long distance," she shot back, wondering why he thought she was unique, but afraid to ask for fear she wouldn't like the answer.

"Pity. Nothing has the personal touch anymore. What were you doing in my study?"

Eleanore blinked, taken aback by the abrupt hardening of his voice. "I didn't realize it was off-limits," she said stiffly. "You may rest assured that I won't trespass again."

"That doesn't answer my question. Why did you come in here?" He eyed her narrowly, wondering if one of his staff had spun her a sob story to enlist her help to rifle his desk. With her soft heart, she'd be a pushover.

"I was planning on robbing the safe, of course, and absconding with my ill-gotten gains," she mocked.

"You haven't got a hope in hell of escaping me, Eleanore Fulton," Murad responded calmly. "But that still doesn't answer my question."

"It doesn't deserve an answer."

"We rarely get what we deserve in this life. Now out with it. What are you doing in here?"

"Oh, for heaven's sake." Eleanore grimaced, suddenly feeling overwhelmingly tired. "I was simply returning the necklace I'd borrowed from you. Wilkerson thought that you'd taken Sonia home so I didn't think I'd be bothering you."

But she did bother him, Murad thought. He found himself constantly being distracted by what she said and did . . . and thought, he admitted. He'd seen the disappointment in her eyes earlier tonight when he'd ignored Walton's insults. For a second he'd been tempted to slip out of the role of a harmless playboy and deal with Walton as he deserved to be dealt with. It was an impulse he'd swiftly repressed. He'd worked too long and hard to slip up now simply to impress a woman, even one as unusual as Eleanore.

"Come here and I'll unfasten the necklace for you," Murad offered.

Eleanore studied him uncertainly. His tone had been almost indulgent. Apparently, she was to be forgiven for trespassing. She walked over to him, the thick pile of the carpet tickling the bottoms of her stockinged feet. Reaching him, she turned around and swept her tumbled curls off her neck. She felt his fingers brush her skin as he picked up the clasp of the necklace and his warm breath wafted across the nape of her neck, electrifying the tiny hairs.

Eleanore tensed as she felt his warm lips moving on her sensitive skin. A rushing torrent of sensation cascaded through her, disrupting her breathing and tying her stomach in knots.

"What are you doing?" Her voice sounded high and breathless.

"Counting these cute little vertebrae that stick up when you bend your neck." His husky voice seemed to be coming from a distance.

"Vertebrae?" The word ended on a breathless sigh as his lips began to nuzzle the hypersensitive skin behind her right ear. A series of tremors shook her and her knees seemed to be having trouble supporting her.

Murad's arm encircled her rib cage and he pulled her back against his body. Eleanore could feel the sinewy hardness of his well-muscled forearm pressing against the bottom of her breasts.

A gasp of longing escaped her as he slowly turned her toward him. His firm lips met hers with the physical impact of a blow, forcing the air from her lungs. She was being inundated by myriad sensations: by the coffee-flavored taste of his mouth, by the enveloping heat of his body and by the pressure of his arms binding her closer to the hardness of his thighs.

Desire such as she'd never experienced washed over her in waves and she mindlessly pressed closer to him. As if encouraged by her spontaneous response, Murad speared his fingers through her tumbled curls, holding her head still as his mouth exerted pressure. Obediently, her lips parted and his tongue triumphantly surged between them to explore the softness of her inner cheek, the hard line of her teeth and the curling edge of her tongue.

The sounds of bells ringing in her ears suddenly registered as the phone and she moaned in denial of anything that would disrupt the exquisite sensations coursing through her.

"I know, my sweet," Murad murmured against her throbbing lips, "but I have to answer it. Everyone in the house knows I'm in here." He picked up the phone.

And everyone probably had a pretty good idea what they were doing in here, too, Eleanore thought, bothered more by her mindless response to him than by their lack of privacy. It was unlike her to react to a kiss so totally, and she found the experience vaguely threatening.

She gave Murad an unsteady smile and beat a hasty retreat. She needed time to think. Time to try to put what she'd felt into some kind of perspective.

7

"THERE'S A SWEET LAMB." Eleanore nuzzled Lacey's cheek, and was rewarded by a happy chortle. She deftly placed the baby in her crib and, with a final caress on her fuzzy head, pulled the blanket up under Lacey's chin. "Have a good nap, angel, and this afternoon you and I will go for a long walk in this gorgeous fall sunshine."

Miss Kelvington nodded approvingly at Eleanore's plans. "What time would you like me to have her ready, Miss Fulton?"

"I have a couple of errands to run this morning, but I should be back in time to give her her noon bottle. Then I'll take charge of her from then until tomorrow."

"It isn't my regular evening off," Miss Kelvington reminded her.

"I know, but I like taking care of Lacey and I don't have anything else planned."

"I'll see you at lunch." Eleanore gave Miss Kelvington a preoccupied smile as she left, busily planning her morning.

First, she'd find out if Kelly had shown up at the college for registration. Then she intended to stop by Barbra's again to see if Kelly had been in touch with her. She wondered if she should check to make sure that the remnants of last night's party had been cleared away before she left, or if that would be considered presumptuous. She didn't want to give Murad reason to complain that she wasn't fulfilling her part of the bargain, but on the other hand, she didn't want him to think she was trying to take over his domestic arrangements. The way a wife might do.

She came to a sudden halt halfway down the front stairs as a searing heat engulfed her at the very thought of being Murad's wife. Of being free to kiss him whenever she wanted. Of being free to run her fingers through his crisp, black hair. Of being free to caress—

"Are you all right, Miss Eleanore?" Wilkerson's deep voice intruded on her fantasy.

"What?" She stared blankly at the butler and then flushed as she realized what she was doing. "I'm fine," she said, although she was beginning to harbor some doubts. It wasn't like her to indulge in daydreams. But then nothing had been normal since she'd met Murad.

She skipped down the last few steps. "I'm going out for a few hours, Wilkerson, if anyone should ask." Surreptitiously, she peeked into the double living room as she passed it. It was absolutely spotless.

"Very nice," she approved. "And very quick."

"Certainly." Wilkerson looked faintly offended that she should even consider otherwise, but Eleanore didn't pause to placate him. She'd suddenly remembered her gorgeous silver sandals and the high-handed way Murad had flung them into his wastebasket. As efficient as the staff was, she'd better rescue them before they were tossed out.

The door to Murad's study was ajar and she boldly walked in, only to come to a dismayed halt as she saw Murad sitting on the edge of his desk, murmuring into the phone.

WOW!

THE MOST GENEROUS
FREE OFFER EVER!

From the Harlequin Reader Service

GET 4 FREE BOOKS WORTH $10.60

Affix peel-off stickers to reply card

FOUR FREE BOOKS

FOUR FREE BOOKS

PLUS A FREE ACRYLIC CLOCK/CALENDAR

AND A FREE MYSTERY GIFT!

NO COST! NO OBLIGATION TO BUY!
NO PURCHASE NECESSARY!

Because you're a reader of Harlequin romances, the publishers would like you to accept four brand-new Harlequin Temptation® novels, with their compliments. Accepting this offer places you under no obligation to purchase any books, ever!

ACCEPT FOUR BRAND-NEW

YOURS

We'd like to send you four free Harlequin novels, worth $10.60, to introduce you to the benefits of the Harlequin Reader Service. We hope your free books will convince you to subscribe, but that's up to you. Accepting them places you under no obligation to buy anything, but we hope you'll want to continue your membership in the Reader Service.

So unless we hear from you, once a month we'll send you four additional Harlequin Temptation® novels to read and enjoy. If you choose to keep them, you'll pay just $2.39* per volume—a savings of 26¢ off the cover price, plus only 49¢ shipping and handling for the entire shipment! There are no hidden extras! And you may cancel at any time, for any reason, just by sending us a note or a shipping statement marked "cancel." You can even return an unopened shipment to us at our expense. Either way the free books and gifts are yours to keep!

ALSO FREE!
ACRYLIC DIGITAL CLOCK/CALENDAR

As a free gift simply to thank you for accepting four free books we'll send you this stylish digital quartz clock— a handsome addition to any decor!

Crystal acrylic case looks good in home or office setting.

Changeable month-at-a-glance calendar pops out; may be replaced with a favorite photograph!

Battery included!

Quartz movement for exceptional accuracy.

*Terms and prices subject to change without notice.

HARLEQUIN TEMPTATION® NOVELS

FREE!

Harlequin Reader Service®

```
AFFIX
FOUR FREE BOOKS
STICKER HERE
```

YES, send me my free books and gifts as explained on the opposite page. I have affixed my "free books" sticker above and my two "free gift" stickers below. I understand that accepting these books and gifts places me under no obligation ever to buy any books; I may cancel at any time, for any reason, and the free books and gifts will be mine to keep!

342 CIH ZDFW

NAME

(PLEASE PRINT)

ADDRESS _____ APT. _____

CITY

PROV. _____ POSTAL CODE

Offer limited to one per household and not valid to current
Harlequin Temptation subscribers. All orders subject to approval.

```
AFFIX FREE
CLOCK/CALENDAR
STICKER HERE
```

```
AFFIX FREE
MYSTERY GIFT
STICKER HERE
```

WE EVEN PROVIDE FREE POSTAGE!

It costs you *nothing* to send for your free books — we've paid the postage on the attached reply card. And we'll pick up the postage on your shipment of free books and gifts!

A muffled sound of annoyance escaped her. She hated being caught barging into his study after her assurances last night that she wouldn't do so. She tried to retreat, but Murad gestured for her to come into the room.

Deciding her best bet would be to act as if she had every right to be here, she walked over to his desk. She searched Murad's face for a clue to his mood. He hadn't been at breakfast earlier and she'd assumed that he'd gone in to work early.

"Here." Murad handed the phone to her.

Eleanore automatically accepted it. "Who is it?" she mouthed.

"Your father."

"My..." She hastily covered the mouthpiece and said, "I don't want to talk to him."

"Life's full of things we don't want to do."

"Ha! Listen to the consummate hedonist," she scoffed. "You can tell my *dear* father—"

"No, you tell him." Murad refused to accept the receiver she shoved at him. "You made a bargain with me. Is your word worth nothing?"

"Oh, all right," she snapped, stung by his charge. "But I didn't say I'd be polite to him."

"You haven't got it in you to be unkind. Would you like me to leave?"

"No," she muttered. Murad might exasperate her, but he also imparted a feeling of security, of strength, for her to draw on.

Taking a deep breath, she gingerly put the receiver to her ear and said, "Hello?"

A very faintly accented voice queried tentatively, "Eleanore?"

"Yes, I'm Eleanore Fulton." She was surprised at the hesitant quality of the man's voice. She'd been expecting an older, more arrogant version of Murad.

"I'm your father, Selim al-Rashid..." His voice trailed off.

Eleanore listened to the silence, wondering if it was worth breaking. But what could she say? Where were you when I was a child? When I used to dream about having parents to take to school open houses like the other kids?

"I'd very much like to see you," Selim finally said.

"Why?" she asked bluntly.

"You are my daughter."

"A fact you've managed to ignore for nearly thirty years."

"There were circumstances," he said slowly.

"Yes, you didn't want to upset the great love of your life. It's a shame you didn't remember your fiancée before you seduced my mother."

"Murad said you were bitter, but I'd hoped...." Selim suddenly sounded old. Old and very tired, and Eleanore felt ashamed of herself for baiting him.

"I'm sorry. I didn't mean to be unkind. Well, maybe I did," she admitted honestly. "But, don't you see? It's too late. It was too late the moment you made the choice to abandon me."

"No," Selim insisted. "I made the choice to have you raised apart from me. But at no time did I abandon you. You have always held a place in my heart, in my prayers, and in my monetary obligations."

"So Murad claims. Exactly what is it you want from me?" she demanded.

"You are my daughter," Selim repeated.

"So we share a blood tie, but that's all we share," Eleanore insisted. "When you returned home to Abar thirty years ago, you left me to be raised in a different culture. We don't have any common meeting ground."

He unexpectedly chuckled. "We have a whole gene pool in common. And the older I get the more important I realize heredity to be. Eleanore, child, I'm not trying to take over your life. All I'm asking is for you not to shut me out."

Like you did me, she thought bitterly, but she couldn't bring herself to fling the hurtful words at him. There had already been so much pain. Maybe Murad was right. Maybe it was time to look ahead instead of back.

"Eleanore?" Selim prompted.

"I'm not making any promises, but I suppose we could get acquainted."

"Thank you, I—" his voice broke. "I'll be in touch." He hung up.

Eleanore slowly replaced the receiver, wishing she could be sure she'd done the right thing.

"Don't look so worried." Murad closed the door, crossed the room and scooped her up into his arms. Eleanore clutched at his suit jacket to steady herself as he walked to the oversize leather chair beside the fireplace and sank down in it.

She didn't know why he'd picked her up, nor did she particularly care. All she knew was that she was where she wanted to be, safe in his arms. With a sigh, she snuggled against his chest, seeking the warmth of his body as a palliative to the cold that filled her.

"The first step is always the hardest," Murad murmured encouragingly, but Eleanore barely heard him.

She was too busy savoring the feel of his fingers as they slipped inside the loose neckline of her emerald silk blouse and began to massage her tight muscles.

"Relax," he whispered. "Take a deep breath and relax." He pulled her blouse out of her slacks and, slipping his hand beneath it, began to rub her back.

Eleanore closed her eyes and nestled closer to him. His hand continued its caressing movement, leaving a burning heat in its wake. She felt disoriented, dizzy and very, very hungry. Her hands went to his chest and, shoving his soft silk tie aside, she unbuttoned his crisp cotton shirt with fingers made clumsy by the strength of her desire. She pushed her hand beneath his shirt and the roughness of his thick body hair across her palm sent a spurt of adrenaline racing through her veins.

"Eleanore!" Murad's hoarse whisper brought a satisfied smile to her lips. He most definitely wasn't immune to her. The knowledge lent her confidence and she bent her head to press small, searching kisses over his chest. She was so absorbed in the feel of his hard thighs beneath her soft hips and in the sound of his harsh breathing echoing in her ears that she didn't notice when he deftly unfastened her bra.

He turned her face up to his and leaned toward her, fitting his lips to hers. He pressed and Eleanore opened her mouth, shivering as his tongue plunged inside with a hunger he made no attempt to disguise.

Eleanore grasped the back of his neck, pulling him closer, eager to savor every nuance of their embrace.

She tensed as she felt the tips of his fingers brush across her now bare breasts and then began to tremble uncontrollably as his hand boldly cupped her.

He rubbed his thumb across the beaded tip and the ache in her loins became unbearable. Blindly, she pressed against his hand to intensify the sensation.

To her bewilderment, Murad raised his head and glared at the closed door.

She followed his frustrated gaze, blinking to bring her eyes into focus. Someone was knocking on the door, she finally realized.

"That special delivery letter you were waiting for has just arrived, Your Excellency." Wilkerson called through the closed door.

"Thank you, Wilkerson. I'll get it before I go." Murad's clipped words constituted a clear dismissal.

"This place makes Grand Central Station look like a country crossroads," Murad snapped, his voice husky with thwarted desire.

"At least he knocked instead of just walking in," Eleanore said thankfully.

"That's because he knows it's more than his job's worth to open a door without permission."

Eleanore shivered slightly at his harsh tone, and Murad's arms tightened comfortingly around her.

"Sorry, Eleanore. I guess we're both a little tense. Take it easy a minute before you get up." He tucked her head beneath his chin and began to rub her back in what he obviously thought was a soothing motion. It wasn't. All it did was feed her already rioting sense of excitement.

She took a deep breath and tried to relax her taut muscles. She had to get a grip on her runaway response before Murad realized just how totally she'd abandoned herself to his kiss. It was as if he had some-

how found a way to tap into a part of her that she hadn't
even known existed. She sighed uneasily.

"Don't worry about meeting Selim." Murad misinterpreted her sigh. He deftly rebuttoned her blouse and
with a quick kiss on her forehead, set her on her feet.

She forced herself to meet his gleaming black eyes
despite the fact that he made her feel shy and unsure of
herself.

"Just meet your father without prejudice and give
yourself a chance to get to know him."

"I'll try, but the past keeps getting caught up in the
present."

"No, your interpretation of the past," Murad corrected.

"The truth is the truth."

"But whose truth? Yours? Your father's? Your mother's? Amineh's?" Murad leaned over and pulled open
the bottom desk drawer.

Eleanore watched in fascination as the muscles in his
back rippled. Straightening up, he tossed a folder onto
the desktop.

"What's that?" she asked.

"Proof of Selim's claim that he didn't simply abandon you."

"I don't want to see it."

"You mean you don't want to grow up! You'd prefer
to stay a child where everything is black and white. Life
isn't like that, Eleanore. It's mostly a spectrum of grays."

"All right! I'll read it! Are you satisfied?"

"No," he said slowly, "but I will be."

Eleanore blinked at the tiny silver lights exploding in
his night-dark eyes. She had the unsettling feeling that

his frame of reference was entirely different from her own.

"Feel free to use the study." He glanced at his watch. "I have to leave. I'm already late for an appointment."

The word "study" triggered her memory as to why she'd come in here in the first place and she said, "I only came in for my shoes. Where are they?"

"What?" Murad looked confused at her sudden change of topic.

"I want my silver sandals."

"Those things aren't shoes. They're an accident waiting to happen."

She sniffed disparagingly. "You simply have no concept of fashionable footwear."

"Possibly," he conceded. "But in any case it's too late. They went out with the morning trash."

"Don't you think you were just the slightest bit high-handed?" she asked in annoyance.

"No, or I wouldn't have done it." His reasoning amused her despite the loss of her gorgeous sandals. Obviously sarcasm was wasted on him.

"Tell you what, Eleanore, if you're that set on silver sandals, I'll pick out a suitable pair for you."

"Impossible," she grumbled. "They don't make orthopedic shoes in silver."

"They make anything if you've got enough money," he said cynically, then paused and gave her a thoughtful look. "I'd be glad to go over the contents of the envelope with you. We could—"

"No, thank you," she said hastily. If there was any truth in what Murad was saying, she didn't want to uncover it under his critical eye. He'd shown only too clearly where his sympathies lay. He'd never give her mother the benefit of the doubt.

"Very well, my prickly little hedgehog. I'll see you this evening."

Hedgehog? Uncertainly, she watched Murad leave. Was that how he saw her? Sharp and defensive? She sighed. She wasn't like that. Not really. It was just that he made her feel so . . .She sank down in his desk chair and closed her eyes, trying to label the assortment of emotions she experienced around him. Finally she decided on excited. Around him she felt as if something truly stupendous were about to happen. As if she were standing on the threshold of some tremendous discovery.

But that didn't really explain why her response to his slightest touch was so volatile. It wasn't as if she'd never been kissed before. Perhaps his touch felt so different because of the trappings of wealth that surrounded him. She glanced around the elegantly furnished room, then rejected the idea. Murad appealed to her in spite of his almost indecent resources, not because of them.

She grimaced, filing the puzzle away to be considered later, when she had more time. She had a lot to do this morning. And Murad had just added one more thing to her list. She eyed the manila folder. She'd promised she'd look at it and she would, but that didn't mean that she had to linger over it.

Opening it, she dumped the contents on the desk and began to sift through what were mostly canceled checks. She glanced at several randomly. One of them was dated the month before her birth. A couple had coffee rings on them.

Eleanore frowned as her mind obligingly supplied a memory of her Aunt Theresa complaining of Marilyn's habit of setting over-full cups of coffee on whatever was available. With a feeling of dread, she reached for a pack of letters held together with a rubber band.

They were all addressed to her father and all bore a return address with her mother's name on it. Some of the addresses she recognized, some she didn't. Opening one, she began to read it.

It was a report on how she, Eleanore, was doing at her private high school and how she wanted to add ballet lessons to the private lessons in horseback riding, swimming and deportment she was already receiving.

Deportment! Eleanore's eyes widened in disbelief. The overcrowded, understaffed public high school she'd gone to wouldn't have known the meaning of the word deportment.

She found the one with the most recent postmark and began to read it. It was a masterfully written piece of fiction, outlining how Eleanore had supposedly fallen in love with some young man who was willing to overlook her irregular birth if her dowry was large enough.

Eleanore's hand involuntarily clenched, crumpling the paper. Despite her taunt to Murad that the checks were forgeries, she knew they weren't. Not only was her mother's rather florid handwriting distinctive, but her method of punctuation was unique.

Eleanore stood up and rubbed her hands over her slacks as if to remove all traces of her contact with the letters.

It was too bad her mother was dead, she thought grimly, because she'd have liked the pleasure of telling

her exactly what she thought of her. Not that it would
have done any good. Anyone as incredibly selfish as her
mother must have been would hardly be swayed by her
rejected daughter's opinion.

And she had been rejected. A pervading sense of hurt
filled her. All her life she'd believed that if her mother
could have kept her, she would have. And now she no
longer had even that comfort. To her mother, she'd
simply been the means to extort money from Selim.
Before she'd read those letters, her mother's rejection
of her had been impersonal, caused by economic forces
outside Marilyn's control. But now that same rejection
had suddenly become very personal, as if her mother
had decided that Eleanore had no value other than as
a source of income.

Eleanore swallowed the tears clogging her throat and
bundled the papers back into the envelope, dropping it
into the desk drawer from which Murad had taken it.

It represented the past and right now, she told her-
self, she had to be more concerned with the present.
And finding Kelly headed her list of present concerns.
She'd . . . She paused as someone knocked on the door.
Hastily rubbing the tears from her cheeks, she shoved
the desk drawer closed and said, "Come in."

Wilkerson opened the door. "I was wondering
whether you would be wanting a driver this morning,
Miss Eleanore? His Excellency said—" Wilkerson unexpectedly grimaced in annoyance.

Fascinated by the show of emotion on his normally
expressionless face, Eleanore asked, "What's wrong?"

"His Excellency's letter." Wilkerson picked up the
envelope from the table just outside the door where he'd
placed it earlier. "I know he wanted it because he de-

layed going in to the office this morning until it came. And then he went off and forgot it." He gave Eleanore a reproachful look, and to her annoyance, she felt a flush redden her pale skin even though she knew it hadn't been her fault he'd forgotten it. Simply because the kiss they'd shared had thrown her off balance was no reason to assume it had had a similar effect on Murad.

"Perhaps Ali could take it over to him?" she suggested.

"Ali flew to Abar last night. Something about a crisis in the oil cartel."

"Well, send it over to him by car. I don't need a driver. Not in the daytime."

"I would, but I'm not sure how important whatever is in the letter is, or how trustworthy the driver is."

"You were going to send me out with him," she said dryly.

"That's hardly the same thing," Wilkerson stated. "Since you're going out anyway, would you mind stopping by His Excellency's office and giving it to him?"

"But I don't know where his office is." She didn't want to face Murad so soon after having discovered the truth about her mother. She needed time to come to terms with the information first.

"The driver does," Wilkerson replied. "It wouldn't take long, and I'm sure you'd be glad to do a favor for His Excellency."

"Of course," she said, giving in gracefully. "But first, I need to make a phone call. Would you please ask the driver to meet me out front in ten minutes."

"Certainly, Miss Eleanore. And thank you." Wilkerson handed her the envelope and left.

Eleanore stuffed it in her purse as she hastily revised her plans for the morning. On her way to Murad's office, she would stop by the college's admissions office to see if Kelly had registered, but instead of visiting Barbra in person, she'd phone her.

Taking a thin handkerchief out of her purse, she put it over the receiver to disguise her voice. Barbra was much more likely to cooperate with a stranger than with her.

Dialing the number, Eleanore waited until Barbra had barked a grumpy hello into the phone and then with a slightly nasal intonation, asked to speak to Kelly.

"Kelly?" Barbra said suspiciously. "She doesn't live here. Who is this?"

"Ms Fellows at the college administrations office," Eleanore lied. "And I am aware she doesn't live with you. She lives with..." Eleanore held the phone near the Wall Street Journal on the desk and riffled the pages to make it sound as though she was searching through a stack of papers. "She lives with a Ms Fulton. But no one answers at that number, and she listed yours as an emergency number. She hasn't enrolled yet and we need to know if she intends to. We really can't continue to hold her place." Eleanore tried to inject a whiny note into her voice.

"I haven't seen her in months," Barbra said. "But if she calls, I'll give her your message."

"Thank you," Eleanore said and hung up, feeling frustrated. Where could her scatterbrained cousin be? Unfortunately, the possibilities for disappearing in New York City were endless.

Picking up her purse, she headed toward the front door, mentally rehearsing what she'd say to the college offices in order to gain the information she wanted.

As it turned out, she was given very little opportunity to say anything. The harried clerk in the admissions office gave her a five-minute lecture on Kelly's irresponsibility for failing to show up for registration, as well as a warning that both the grant the college had arranged to cover her tuition and her place in the freshman class would be given to another, presumably more conscientious, student if Kelly didn't present herself to the Registrar shortly.

Promising to produce Kelly, even though she didn't have the vaguest idea how she was going to accomplish it, Eleanore escaped.

She was not in a congenial frame of mind by the time she reached Murad's office. Her disappointment over still having no solid leads to Kelly's whereabouts, combined with the shock of finding out about her mother's duplicity, had left her feeling emotionally wrung out. She felt as if she were teetering on the edge of a precipice and any sudden movement would send her hurtling into a void.

"His Excellency's offices are located on the twenty-ninth floor," the driver informed her in a heavily accented voice. "Would you prefer to go up yourself or would you like me to park in the underground lot and escort you?"

"Just let me out, please. I'll take a cab home."

"As you wish, Miss Fulton." He double-parked the Rolls by the front entrance, got out and opened the door for her.

"Thank you," Eleanore said absently, excitement beginning to bubble through her at the thought of seeing Murad. She hurried through the plate-glass doors and across the three-story lobby toward the bank of elevators on the far wall.

Once on the twenty-ninth floor, it was a simple matter to find Murad's investment firm. She opened the heavy oak door and found herself in a spacious reception room that looked more like the living room of a luxurious private home than a business office.

A pretty young woman greeted her from the reception desk to the right of the door. "May I help you, Miss Fulton?"

"Good morning—" Eleanore searched her memory and came up with a name "—Angela. I'm here to see His Excellency. If you could simply point me in the direction of his office?"

Eleanore's eyes narrowed as she watched the woman surreptitiously depress a button on the elaborate intercom system on her desk. So Murad had left orders he was to be warned of unexpected visitors. But why?

"His office is the first one on the right. Through there." She pointed to the far hall.

"Thank you." Eleanore gave her a polite smile and moved toward the hallway.

8

ELEANORE WAS ABOUT TO KNOCK on Murad's door when the door across the way suddenly opened.

"Good morning, Miss Fulton. I wouldn't have expected to see your lovely face here so early after last night's party." Mr. Walton's voice held a question.

"No?" Eleanore eyed him speculatively. So the receptionist's warning hadn't been for Murad. It had been for Walton. Did he check out all visitors to the office or simply all of Murad's? Whichever it was, Eleanore felt it was exceedingly presumptuous of him.

"I'm a lot sturdier than I look. And apparently, a lot smarter. Why are you trying to intercept Murad's visitors?" she asked bluntly.

"Is that what I was doing?" He gave her a look of wide-eyed innocence that Sonia might have been able to pull off. It made him look like a pop-eyed frog.

"I watched the receptionist signal you."

"How observant of you."

"Yes, wasn't it," she agreed with a bland smile. "Also persistent. Why are you spying on Murad's visitors?"

"Really, Miss Fulton, I must protest your unfortunate choice of words. I don't spy. As the director of this office—"

"Co-director."

"My aim is the smooth running of this office." He ignored her correction. "And it will run so much more smoothly if I can head off all the women who are forever chasing after His Excellency. He's such a popular man. But then money does that."

"Yes," Eleanore said levelly. "And the fact that he's handsome, well-mannered and charming doesn't hurt either."

"My dear Miss Fulton, I feel it my duty to warn you—"

"Duty, hell!" Eleanore snapped. "You're trying to cause trouble for your own ends and I'm not taking the bait."

"You may think having had his kid will protect you, but—"

"No, what will protect me is my father, Selim al-Rashid."

"You're lying." Walton looked shaken. "I've dealt with al-Rashid for years and he doesn't have any children."

"Not legitimate. But now that his wife is dead, he has no qualms about recognizing me."

"It doesn't matter," Walton said. "This is the Ahiqar family business and Murad doesn't care enough about anything to take the trouble to defend you."

"Oh, but I'm counting on his disinterest." Eleanore carried the attack into Walton's camp.

"What!" He looked taken aback.

"Counting on the fact that he won't care enough about the business to defend you when I start pushing him to get rid of you. If you're right, he should simply let me have my way to avoid any unpleasantness. And I can be very unpleasant." Her voice hardened. "Now, if you will excuse me...."

To her relief he stalked back into his office, slamming the door behind him. She let her breath out in a long, shaky sigh, feeling unnerved by the encounter. Unnerved and more than a little ashamed at how quick she'd been to use her father's name to her own advantage when up to now she'd been self-righteous about refusing to have anything to do with him. But it had not just been to protect herself, she admitted. It had been Walton's snide cracks about Murad that had annoyed her the most.

With a perfunctory knock, she pushed open Murad's door to find him leaning over a flustered-looking Beth who was sitting in his desk chair, a notepad and pencil held limply in her hands.

They both looked up as she walked in and Beth's expression of guilt combined with Murad's look of shocked surprise would have been hilarious if she had been in the mood to be amused. Unfortunately, she wasn't. She was thoroughly confused. What was going on? At first glance it appeared that Murad was having a go at seducing Beth, but that made no sense. While she didn't doubt that he had playboy tendencies, she'd seen absolutely no evidence that he played with youthful innocents, which was most definitely what Beth was. Either Murad was a closet satyr or something very strange was going on.

"Oh, Eleanore . . . we didn't . . . I mean . . ." Beth shot her a pleading look. "I'll type these letters, Your Excellency," she gasped and scurried out of the room.

"Really, Eleanore," Murad sounded bored. "You shouldn't frighten the staff. It makes for bad labor relations."

"The emphasis being on relations, no doubt!" Her curiosity was beginning to be replaced by annoyance. She'd seen Murad in many different moods since she'd moved into his house, but this was the first time she'd seen him in the role of bored sophisticate. She didn't like it.

"Don't worry, I won't be here long enough to cramp your style." She opened her purse and started to pull out the special-delivery letter he'd forgotten. "I only wanted to bring you—"

To her dumbfounded amazement, he sprinted across the room, grabbed her in his arms and covered her mouth with his. The hard pressure of his lips was echoed in the fierce pressure of his arms holding her immobile against his chest. His tongue pressed against her lips demanding admission, and Eleanore automatically parted them, only realizing her tactical error when his tongue surged inside.

She tried to think, but the sensuous stroke of his thrusting tongue in the warm cavern of her mouth made it very difficult for her to do anything except feel.

"Oh, excuse me, Your Excellency." Walton's voice from the doorway echoed triumphantly in Eleanore's sensitive ears. "I didn't realize that you were occupied."

"Well, now that you do, suppose you leave." Murad's amused voice added to Eleanore's confusion. What was going on? She tried to move away, but Murad's arms tightened, holding her trapped against him.

As soon as the door closed behind Walton, Murad whispered in her ear, "Don't say anything. The room's bugged."

Her eyes widened in disbelief and she stared into his frowning face. The amusement he'd just shown Walton had disappeared as if eliminated by an eraser.

He took the letter she held crushed in her fingers and slipped it into his inside suit pocket.

Walking over to the desk, he began to rummage through the papers there. "Tell you what, darling, I'll take you shopping. You'd like that, wouldn't you?" He turned and nodded at her.

Was that her cue? she wondered. Murad couldn't seriously believe that the room was bugged, could he? She peered uncertainly at him, shivering slightly at the hard gleam in his eyes. This was the Murad who'd rescued her from the mugger, not the casually sophisticated man she normally dealt with.

Great, she thought in exasperation. Just what she needed. A paranoid host who was into spy movies.

"We could do our shopping at Cartier's, if you like." Murad's coaxing tone was totally at variance with his frown of annoyance at her failure to play along.

Why not, she decided. She'd always liked cops and robbers as a kid. The only thing that bothered her was not knowing which category she fell into!

"What a lovely idea," she cooed. "I definitely think I deserve something for my jewelry box after the shock I've just had."

Murad sent her a warning look. "Wait till we get home, darling. I'll make it all up to you. Come along." He took her arm.

Eleanore managed to contain her curiosity until Murad had maneuvered his silver Jaguar XKE into the heavy morning traffic. "All right, spill it," she demanded.

"Spill it?" Murad gave her an innocent look.

"Oh, no, you don't. You can't claim spies in the closet and then try to pretend you didn't say it."

"Spies? Who said anything about spies?"

"You said your office was bugged."

"And so it is. There's one in the phone, one in the base of the lamp, and one behind the picture above the sofa."

"Behind the picture! Your spy has no more imagination than you do," she said. "Tell me, if you know that the listening devices are there, why don't you simply remove them?"

"You have no head for intrigue," Murad said pityingly.

"Sorry. I've led a rather conventional life. It took you to introduce me to espionage."

"There are many things I'd like to introduce you to, Eleanore." Murad gently traced her earlobe with his fingertip.

Trying to ignore the cascade of shivers his gentle caress sent coursing over her skin, Eleanore said, "Facts now, flirt later."

"I can't distract you?" He shifted gears at the changing light.

Couldn't he just, she thought ruefully, but if he didn't already realize just how sensitized she was becoming to his touch, she had no intention of enlightening him.

"I want to know about your spies," she insisted.

Murad frowned, not wanting to involve her directly in his pursuit of the thief. Unfortunately, by bringing that letter to his office she'd taken the decision out of his hands. A reluctant smile teased his lips at her determined expression. She wasn't going to be fobbed off with a facile lie. And that being the case, he might as well tell her the whole thing, he decided. As sharp as she was, she just might catch something that he'd missed.

"They aren't spies. They're thieves," he said.

"Thieves bugged your office?"

"Maybe. Maybe not." Murad shrugged. "It's more likely it was done by Walton in order to keep track of what I'm doing."

"That I'll buy. That sneaky little toad was trying to convince me that you were a compulsive womanizer. And then, of course, I walked in on you coming on to Beth."

"Only because you said she was in love with Abrams. And if she's in love with another man, she isn't going to take me seriously."

"Then why do it? No." She held up her hand as he started to say something. "This is getting me nowhere. I'll ask questions. You answer them."

"That depends on the questions."

"First of all, if you've got thieves, something's being stolen, right?"

"A brilliant piece of deduction." He gave her a sardonic smile.

"Watch the traffic," she said. "What's being stolen?"

"Information about which pieces of property our office is about to buy. The thief nips in, buys a crucially located piece of land and sells it back to us at an exorbitant price."

"Not under his own name, I take it?"

"He uses a dummy corporation and the money is deposited directly into a numbered Swiss bank account."

"Who makes the decisions on what to buy?"

"Walton and Talbort."

"Then one of them has to be your thief. Right?"

"Wrong. It could also be someone with access to their information."

"Which widens the field considerably," Eleanore conceded. "Personally, I like Walton as the villain of the piece. I think that man would stoop to anything."

"Possibly, but from what I've seen, being in charge is an obsession with him. He constantly manipulates the staff and when he finds one who won't be manipulated, he gets rid of them."

"Gets rid of them?" Eleanore's eyes widened in horror.

"Fires them," Murad elaborated. "That's why I lean toward him as the one responsible for the bugs in my office. He views my appearance on the scene as a threat to his supremacy and he wants advance notice of anything I may be planning."

"And you're acting like an adolescent drowning in his own hormones in order to lull the thief into a false sense of security?"

"Ouch." Murad winced. "And here I thought I was portraying a sophisticated man of the world."

"Sophisticated men of the world don't drool over vacuous blondes," Eleanore said wryly. "And speaking of Sonia, how's she going to feel when you suddenly drop her?"

"Considerably wealthier. Sonia is, for want of a better term, a money groupie."

"A what?"

"A woman who gets turned on by money. She hangs around men who are willing to lavish it on her in exchange for sexual favors. That's why I chose her as a prop in my role as a playboy. She wouldn't mistake a determined pursuit of her for anything else."

"Murad," Eleanore said slowly, "exactly who are you?"

"My father's youngest son who's been sent to America to run the family investment firm and have a go at catching the thief who's been bleeding said firm."

"But why you?" she persisted.

"Because in outlook I'm the most Americanized. And because I ran our country's information-gathering network for five years," he added reluctantly.

"You mean your country's spy ring."

"Information gathering is not spying," Murad protested.

"A rose by any other name," Eleanore retorted. "Tell me, what have you been able to find out besides the fact that Walton is pathologically jealous of his position?"

"Absolutely nothing," Murad said in frustration. "Nobody in the office spends more than can reasonably be accounted for. No one appears to be being blackmailed. No one even has anything in their past to make them susceptible to being blackmailed."

"Your thief is clever."

"More important, he's patient. He's willing to wait to spend what he's made." Murad sighed.

"Could you try setting a trap? Maybe give out false information and when he acts on it, leave him holding worthless property?"

"To do that, I'd have to take Walton and Talbort into my confidence and since there's an excellent chance one of them is the guilty party..."

"Maybe you could make an arbitrary decision," she improvised. "Kind of along the lines of 'I am the owner of the company and I say we buy this piece of property.'"

"The thief's too clever for that. He's not going to act on anything I might say because he'd be afraid that Walton might talk me out of it."

"That man is a pain in the neck."

"Personally, I'd put it a little more strongly than that," Murad said. "But I can't get rid of him yet."

"Why not?"

"For two reasons. First, I want to keep all the players in place until I solve the crime and, secondly, Walton has worked in my family's best interests for almost fifteen years. The only honorable thing to do is to give him a little time to come to terms with the new setup." Murad smoothly pulled around a taxi that had stopped suddenly.

"This is going to be no fun at all if you're going to start wallowing in noblesse oblige," she complained. "But as for catching your thief, I'd like to help."

"You already are," Murad assured her. "You're doing a marvelous job of reinforcing my image as a good-for-nothing playboy. Do you realize that the entire office thinks Lacey is mine?" He chuckled and Eleanore ran the tip of her tongue over her suddenly dry lips. Warmth engulfed her at the thought of Murad as her lover. Slowly, her eyes closed as she pictured Murad leaning over her, his dark eyes gleaming with desire and his lean features hardened in passion. Passion for her. Eleanore's breath shortened and desire stabbed her.

"Lacey's father must be dark." Murad's voice broke into her erotic fantasy and Eleanore forced open her weighted eyelids and stared blindly at his profile, trying to force her disoriented mind to think. Should she continue the fiction that Lacey was hers or should she tell him the truth? Frantically, she tried to decide what would be the best thing to do.

There was so much more to Murad than she'd originally thought. The shallow pleasure-seeker had turned out to be a highly intelligent, very purposeful man in pursuit of a definite goal. He also appeared to be extremely loyal to both his family and his friends, she thought, remembering his efforts on her father's behalf. Surely, such a man would understand why she'd lied about Lacey. He might even help her find Kelly. She felt a sudden surge of excitement. He'd talked of how much money his employees had spent. Of events in their background for which they might be blackmailed. If he had the resources to discover that kind of information, then finding Kelly should be child's play for him.

Common sense slowly extinguished her first burst of enthusiasm. Just because he could do something, didn't necessarily mean he would. Nor could she be absolutely certain he would continue to provide for Lacey once he discovered who she really was. He might be the most fascinating man she'd ever meet, but there were a lot of unknown facets to his personality. Headed by his Middle Eastern heritage. He might appear to be western, but he wasn't, and every once in a while that fact came through, loud and clear.

Confessing that she'd lied about Lacey was not a step she wanted to take lightly. First she'd weigh her options very carefully and then she'd decide what was the best thing to do.

Murad pulled into the parking area behind his house and leaned across her to open her door. She shivered as his arm brushed against her breasts, holding her body steady with an effort, desperately wanting to lean forward, to savor the sensation of touching him. But she knew that a parked car in broad daylight was not the place to indulge the impulse.

"Out you go." His brisk words shattered the longing that had held her captive.

"Aren't you coming in?"

"No, I need to take care of a few things downtown. I'll see you tonight." In the face of such an obvious dismissal, Eleanore had no choice but to climb out of the car.

Get a grip on yourself, she lectured herself as she crossed the huge, walled garden behind the town house. She knew she was becoming much too interested in what Murad thought and did. Especially in what he did with her. A dreamy expression softened her face as she relived their kiss in his study.

What would it feel like if he were to make love to her? She paused just inside the back door, staring blindly at the heavy cream damask wallpaper. Would he be as demanding in bed as he was out of it? Would he bring the entire force of his vibrant personality to bear on his partner?

"Are you all right, Miss Eleanore?"

Eleanore hastily straightened up at the sound of Wilkerson's concerned voice. "Yes, of course. I was just . . . just thinking about taking Lacey to the park," she improvised. "Is there a car free?"

"Yes, the Rolls has already returned. Were you able to deliver His Excellency's letter?"

"No problem. Would you ask the driver to bring the car around to the front?" She gave him a smile and sprinted up the stairs, eager to collect Lacey and be off. In fact, eager to do anything that would take her mind off Murad and her growing fascination with him.

Contrary to her expectations, her leisurely afternoon with Lacey did not help her unsettled state of mind. If anything, it made matters worse. Eleanore kept finding herself lapsing into impossible daydreams in which Lacey was her baby. Hers and Murad's.

By the time she returned to the house later that afternoon, she was thoroughly out of sorts. Being curious about a man was one thing, becoming obsessed with him was quite another. It didn't help strengthen her precarious composure when she was met at the door by Wilkerson with the information that Murad had been trying to reach her all afternoon.

"Shall I ring him back for you, Miss Eleanore?" Wilkerson asked.

"Please." Eleanore hoped her eagerness wasn't too obvious.

"Here you are." Wilkerson handed her the ringing phone. Eleanore shifted the baby to her left arm and took it.

"Hello?" Murad's deep voice flowed over the wire, further jangling her already agitated nerves.

"It's me. Eleanore. Wilkerson said you wanted me?"

"Darling, I always want you," Murad purred, and Eleanore's heartbeat skyrocketed until she remembered the bug on Murad's phone. Window dressing. That was all his comment was.

"Darling, you're insatiable." Disappointment lent a realistic edge to her voice.

"Only where you're concerned. You hold the key to my heart," he said with such soulful emphasis that she was hard-pressed to keep from giggling. Apparently, there was a lot of ham mixed in with the spy.

"I just called to tell you that we're meeting a colleague of mine at the Plaza for dinner."

"Fine, I—" she broke off with an annoyed exclamation when she remembered the baby. "I'm sorry. I can't come. I gave Miss Kelvington the day off and she's already left the house."

Expecting him to be annoyed, she was surprised at his solution.

"No problem. I'll simply have them serve dinner in a suite. Lacey can sleep in one of the bedrooms and, if she should need you during the evening, you'll be right there."

"It seems like a lot of trouble to go to just to have dinner out," she said doubtfully.

"It's no trouble." Murad brushed off her concern. "I'll meet you at the hotel at eight. Make sure you use a driver."

"I will," she promised. "Bye." Eleanore hung up, full of questions she had wanted to ask, but couldn't because of the bug on his phone. Such as who were they meeting for dinner? Someone connected with the thefts? Or someone with information about them? And why not have dinner here? The caliber of the cooking of the temperamental Gaston was vastly superior to that in most restaurants. Was the house being watched and was Murad afraid someone would recognize his dinner guest? And maybe she was the one with the case of paranoia, she chided herself. What she should be doing was figuring out a way to help Murad solve his crime, instead of indulging in useless speculation.

But how? she wondered as she slowly carried Lacey up to the nursery. What could she do that Murad hadn't already done? She didn't know, but she was certain there was something they were both missing because there was no such thing as a perfect crime.

She still hadn't come up with any ideas by the time the driver dropped her off at the hotel. Snuggling the drowsy baby against the garnet silk of her cocktail dress, Eleanore crossed the luxurious lobby to the desk.

"Yes, ma'am?" The desk clerk gave her a bright, professional smile. "May I help you?"

"I'm supposed to meet Murad Ahiqar here."

"Of course." The man seemed to snap to attention. "His Excellency arrived almost an hour ago. Peter," he nodded toward the bellhop who hurried over, "will take you up to his suite."

"Thank you." Eleanore handed the young man the diaper bag she was carrying and then followed him toward the bank of elevators.

The suite Murad was occupying was located on the twenty-seventh floor at the end of an elegantly decorated hallway.

Curiously, Eleanore looked around the sitting room while Murad handed the bellhop a tip. A dining table had been set up in front of the ceiling-to-floor window that overlooked the Manhattan skyline.

"Poor lamb. She looks as if she's had it." Murad stroked his finger over Lacey's petal-soft cheek, managing to brush against Eleanore's breast in the process.

Eleanore caught her breath in an inaudible gasp at the sudden wave of longing that surged through her. It seemed to her beleaguered senses that every time he touched her, her response came quicker and lasted longer.

"There's a crib in the smaller bedroom. Through there." Murad pointed to the door in the far wall. "Why don't you put her to bed while I make a phone call?"

Eleanore carried Lacey into the bedroom, her eyes widening at the sight of the queen-size bed that dominated the luxurious room. If this was the small bedroom, she'd love to see the large one, Eleanore thought, shuddering at what this suite must cost.

"There you are, angel." Eleanore gently placed the sleeping baby on her stomach in the crib that had been placed between the bed and the wall. The air-conditioning left the room a little chilly for such a small baby so she covered her with the bright blue blanket folded across the railing.

"I have to run down to the lobby," Murad said when she returned to the sitting room. "If my guest should arrive while I'm gone, let him in. I'll be back in a few minutes."

"But . . ." Eleanore found she was protesting to the closing door. "Great," she muttered. How was she supposed to know this guest from anyone who just happened to knock on the door? And not only that, but what was she supposed to talk to him about? So far Murad's business colleagues had fallen into two groups. The Middle-Eastern ones who simply stared at her, seemingly amazed that she would even have an opinion, let alone voice it, and the people from his office who all appeared to be busily grinding axes of their own.

Her hope that Murad would get back before his guest arrived proved futile, as two minutes later there was a gentle rap on the door.

Taking a deep breath, she pinned what she hoped would pass for a welcoming smile on her face and opened the door.

"Yes?" she asked, wanting to make sure the man standing there really was Murad's guest before she invited him in.

"I . . . ah, Murad said . . ." the man stammered, looking distinctly ill at ease.

Oh, great, Eleanore thought in resignation. One of the Middle-Eastern contingent.

"Murad had to leave for a moment, but he'll be right back." *I hope.* "Would you like to come in and wait?"

The man nodded his graying head and moved toward the couch. Eleanore followed, feeling sorry for him. His agitation at finding himself alone with a woman was almost tangible. He simply wasn't ready to be turned loose in western society and Murad should have known it.

"May I get you some coffee?" Eleanore made an effort to put him at ease.

"No. I only wanted . . . that is . . . you're . . ."

Eleanore frowned as a horrible suspicion began to grow in her mind. No businessman could be as socially inept as this man appeared to be, unless he was under a great deal of emotional strain.

Briefly, she closed her eyes in negation of her fears. Surely Murad wouldn't simply spring her father on her like this? Not after she'd told him that she wanted to choose her own time for the meeting.

"E-Eleanore," the man stammered.

"Who are you?" she interrupted.

"Your father. Please." He reached for her, but Eleanore instinctively retreated and his hand dropped limply to his side. "Please don't hate me," he said simply.

"I don't," she said, surprised to find it was true. It had been easy to hate a faceless entity, but she was finding it impossible to hate the real person sitting opposite her. Especially when he looked so desperately unhappy.

"I want us to be a family, Eleanore," he blurted out.

Eleanore stared at him, unable to cruelly rebuff him and equally unable to fall into his arms and pretend that the last thirty years had never happened.

The sound of the door opening seemed very loud in the tense silence and Eleanore turned toward it, her eyes narrowing as she saw Murad. She couldn't wait for the chance to tell him what she thought of his underhanded trick. By the time she got through taking him apart, he'd need his spy network just to find the pieces!

Murad, after a quick glance at her angry features, ignored her. He greeted Selim with pleasure, and immediately directed the conversation into the impersonal and unemotional subject of barrels, ceilings and oil cartels. After a few minutes, Eleanore gave up trying to follow what was being said, and simply allowed her mind to drift, trying very hard to relax.

9

MURAD CLOSED THE DOOR behind Selim and turned to Eleanore. "That wasn't so bad, was it?"

"Wasn't so—" Eleanore yelled, as the intolerable tension of the evening finally snapped. "Why you pompous, overbearing, autocratic, overstuffed—"

"I am not overstuffed!"

"Who the hell gave you the right to play God!"

"It's a big job, but someone's got to do it."

His bad joke was the final straw. Murad had just subjected her to one of the most stressful, emotionally gut-wrenching sessions she'd ever lived through and he thought it was funny! Grimly, she took a deep breath.

"I find your unwarranted interference completely reprehensible." She clearly enunciated each word and then stalked toward the small bedroom. Suddenly remembering that Lacey was asleep in it, she veered toward the second bedroom.

Pushing the door open, she marched inside, blind to the almost oppressive luxury that surrounded her. She had to escape Murad for a few minutes before she gave way to the fury coursing through her and threw something at him. Preferably something hard! For the first time in her life she understood how crimes of passion were committed.

She turned to find that Murad had followed her into the room. The sound of his footsteps had been swallowed up by the thick, white carpeting.

"Go away." She glared at him.

"Eleanore, don't be unreasonable." He reached out, and grasping her nape, gave her a gentle shake. A cascade of sensation washed over her skin and she jerked back, appalled at her reaction. Part of her wanted to annihilate him, but another part wanted to fall into his arms.

"Unreasonable!" She forced herself to focus on her very real grievance. "You go behind my back and do something you knew I didn't want you to do and you have the unmitigated gall to call me unreasonable."

"I know you're angry, Eleanore, but if—"

"And here I thought you weren't a perceptive man."

"If you'd just think about it, you'd realize that what I did was for the best," Murad insisted.

"Whose best? Mine? I think we can dispense with that fiction. Lacey's? Carted across town when she should be in her own bed."

"I carted the pair of you across town, as you so elegantly put it, because I didn't want to invite Selim to my home."

"Oh? Isn't dear Papa socially acceptable?"

"I didn't invite him to my home because at the moment it's also your home." Murad held on to his temper with an almost visible effort. "I didn't want you to feel that you had no control over who came and went in your home. I thought that the hotel would be a neutral site."

"Oh." Eleanore blinked, taken aback by his explanation. It showed a degree of sensitivity that didn't seem to go with his arrogance in setting the meeting up in the first place.

She watched as he ran impatient fingers through his hair, noting the wayward strand that tumbled over his broad forehead. Her fingers itched to push it away, and that made her even angrier. She felt as if Murad was slowly taking control of everything, including her emotions.

"Eleanore, listen to me." He grasped her shoulders.

"No!"

"Yes," he insisted. "Look at this mess from my point of view. Selim leaves for Switzerland tomorrow to represent Abar at a very important OPEC meeting. How is he supposed to do a good job when all he can think about is meeting you? And you won't agree to meet him because you're afraid."

"Afraid!" She took exception to his choice of words.

"Yes, afraid. You're clinging to old grievances because you're afraid to face the future. Maybe I shouldn't have interfered, but basically I'm a man of action and your dithering over something that was going to happen eventually anyway was not only exasperating, it was futile."

"And Selim wanted it, so to hell with what I wanted." To her mortification, she burst into tears.

"Eleanore!" Murad sounded horrified. "It wasn't like that at all." He swept her up into his arms and, carrying her over to the king-size bed, sat down with her on his lap. "I didn't expect you to be this upset. I honestly thought I was simply pushing you off dead center. Please, don't cry, darling." He cradled her head against his chest and began to slowly rub her back.

The warmth generated by his rhythmically moving hand heated the thin silk of her dress, causing it to cling to her skin with tiny sparks of static electricity. Back and forth, his caressing hand moved, tracing up over her rib cage and then down to her waist.

In unconscious negation of an almost overwhelming urge to arch into his hand, she jerked sideways, knocking Murad off balance. His arms automatically tightened around her as he fell backward onto the bed and Eleanore ended up sprawled across him. The feel of his hard body beneath hers shocked her out of her crying.

"My poor put-upon darling." Murad's caressing hand inched downward, massaging the base of her spine.

Eleanore wiggled in response to the hypnotic movement. The front of her skirt had ridden up when she'd fallen and she could feel the slightly scratchy texture of his pants against the sleekness of her panty hose. She flexed her leg slightly and the delectable friction intensified.

Murad rolled onto his side, still holding her captive against him. He began to place tiny kisses along her jawline and Eleanore shivered as the raspy texture of his clean-shaven chin scraped across her neck.

"You're wrong about my arranging this meeting because of concern for Selim." His warm breath wafted across her cheek, causing the soft skin to tighten.

"Murad?" His name came out as an involuntary sigh of longing.

The feel of him was playing havoc with her common sense, dissolving her very real grievance. Somehow, his high-handedness didn't seem quite so important when she was locked in his arms. Later, she decided hazily.

Later, she'd try to make him understand that he didn't have the right to make her decisions for her. Right now, all she wanted to do was to enjoy the sensations he was arousing.

His wandering lips suddenly homed in on hers with a burning male hunger that drove the lingering remnants of their argument from her mind. All she could think about was the need he was making no effort to hide from her. It was a need that found a counterpart in her own throbbing body.

Her fingers clutched his head in an attempt to pull him closer. He didn't come. Instead, he drew back and unfastened the two large buttons that held the front of her dress together. His expression of rapt fascination as he slowly pulled the material back filled her with a sense of awed wonder. That such a sophisticated, worldly man should find her so enthralling gave her a heady sense of feminine power that she'd never felt before.

"Sweet, sweet Eleanore," he whispered as he disposed of her wispy lace bra. "You're even more beautiful than I imagined." Reverently, he covered her small, satiny breasts with slow, languorous kisses.

Eleanore moaned in mindless pleasure as he slowly rubbed his hands over the soft mounds. His palms were rough and sent shards of sensations piercing through her. She squeezed her eyes closed, the better to concentrate on the exquisite feeling.

"At the party the other night I watched your body moving beneath this dress—" his deep voice drew her deeper into the web of desire he was spinning "—and all I could think about was that just two buttons stood between me and my heart's desire. I was on fire to kiss you like this." His mouth suddenly replaced his hand

and he lightly caught the tip of her breast between his strong, white teeth. His tongue scraped across the dusky-rose flesh, convulsing it into a tight bud of desire. For a brief second the uncontrolled rasp of her breathing echoing in her ears cleared her mind enough for her to realize that she was fast approaching the point of no return. Soon she wouldn't care about anything but that he not stop.

"Murad, we can't . . . I'm not . . ." She struggled for words to complete the thought. "I'm not on the pill," she finally blurted out and then buried her face against his shoulder.

"Of course you aren't, my sweet one," he crooned. "Don't worry. I'll take care of it. I'll take care of everything." His fingers lightly traced around the whorls in her ear.

With a sigh of pure pleasure, Eleanore rubbed her hands over the crisp texture of his cotton shirt, then rotated her palms in small circles, exploring the springy texture of the hair on his chest.

Not satisfied with the contact, she fumbled with the buttons on his shirt. She wanted to explore his body as he was exploring hers.

Having no trouble comprehending her purpose, Murad stood up and tore off his clothes, tossing them onto the floor.

Mesmerized, Eleanore watched him, glorying in the magnificence of his lean, muscled body. "You're gorgeous," she murmured wonderingly.

"And you, my lovely, are gorgeous, too." He moved away from her for a moment and then returned, sinking down on the bed beside her. With a slow deliberation that Eleanore found irresistible, he peeled off her panty hose.

Murad's mouth hovered above hers, and the tip of his tongue slowly, tantalizingly stroked over her soft lips.

Eleanore threaded her fingers through his hair, her fingertips pressing against his well-shaped head as she pulled him closer.

"Murad, kiss me," she whispered.

"But where, my lovely?" His husky voice heated her bare skin. "I'm spoiled by choices. Should I kiss your delectable lips?" He punctuated each word with a quick kiss. "They feel like rose petals. Or, perhaps, I should start with your breasts? Or, perhaps..."

She jerked in reaction to the bolt of excitement that shot through her as Murad began to paint intricate designs on her abdomen with his tongue.

"I was wrong," he said reflectively. "Your skin is more like a gardenia, velvety-soft, creamy-white and infinitely fragrant."

Eleanore gasped and her body went rigid as he slipped his hand between them and slowly began to probe the heart of her femininity.

"Murad!" A soft cry tore from her throat as she writhed beneath him.

"That's right, my lovely," he encouraged her. "Just relax and let it happen."

"Relax!" Her voice broke on a jagged sigh of rapture as he slowly began to caress the very core of her desire. Her hips lifted convulsively into the hypnotic movement of his fingers and her breathing developed a ragged cadence.

"Please, Murad." She twisted beneath him. "I can't bear..." Her breath caught as she felt the hard length of him probing her moist softness.

Longingly, she arched upward, desperate to feel him within her. But Murad's hands slipped beneath her hips, holding her back.

"Easy," he growled the word. "I'm teetering on the edge of losing what little control I have left. I want to make this perfect for you."

"Any more perfect and I won't survive," Eleanore gasped. She clutched his lean hips and, digging her heels into the silky, soft comforter, pushed up with all her strength. There was a moment of discomfort as her body struggled to adjust to his overwhelming maleness and then suddenly he filled her, making her whole.

"Yes, oh, yes!" she muttered, her mind focused inward on the burgeoning pressure tightening the coil of desire deep in her abdomen. Deliberately, she gave herself up to the feeling. Being in control didn't seem to matter anymore. All that mattered was that she find an answer to the overwhelming tension that had her in its relentless grip.

She wrapped her legs around his hips, arching her body to meet his deep, powerful thrusts. She felt as if she were riding the crest of an enormous wave, when suddenly it broke and tossed her boneless body into an exploding world of incredible sensation.

Vaguely, as if from a great distance, she heard Murad's hoarse voice as he followed her.

When his labored breathing had finally returned to something approaching normal, he rolled onto his side and, gathering her pliant body against him, tucked her head beneath his chin and murmured, "Go to sleep, Eleanore."

Stunned by the force of her reaction, Eleanore made no attempt to obey him. She simply lay in his arms, trying to keep her chaotic thoughts at bay while she savored the exquisite aftermath of the most incredible experience of her life.

But why had it been? The question nagged at her like an aching tooth. What was it about Murad that had turned what should have been a pleasant physical experience into something that defied description? It made no sense, but the indisputable fact remained that with Murad lovemaking took on dimensions and hues and tones that she hadn't even suspected existed.

And it had been making love. The self-knowledge that had been lapping at the edges of her consciousness for days suddenly burst through the restraint she'd placed on it. Close on its heels came anguish so profound she thought the bleakness of it would freeze her soul.

She didn't need a crystal ball to know there was no future in loving Murad. No vine-covered cottage filled with laughing children. He probably owned a vine-covered castle somewhere, she thought on a flash of bitter humor, but nothing so ordinary as a cottage. Murad was so far outside her normal environment that in the natural order of things, she would never have even met him, let alone gotten to know him well enough to fall in love with him. But maybe she wasn't really in love with him. Maybe she was simply infatuated with him.

She instantly rejected the idea. Infatuation implied a blind acceptance of all aspects of his personality and she didn't do that. She knew every one of his faults. But even his infuriating habit of assuming that he knew best became a minor flaw when compared to his good points: his intelligence, his loyalty, his sense of humor that so surprisingly dovetailed with her own, his gentleness with Lacey, the fact that he truly cared about people and tried to express that concern in a practical manner, his skill as a lover.... She shifted restlessly and Murad's grip tightened.

"Go to sleep, Eleanore," he repeated.

At least he knew who she was, she comforted herself. He hadn't confused her with anyone else. Although, if he were to be believed, and she did believe him, there wasn't anyone else in his life. At least not in any way that counted. But simply because he wasn't involved with another woman didn't mean that he intended to establish an ongoing relationship with her. In fact, she was willing to bet that he hadn't intended to make love to her tonight. It had been her emotional outburst that had triggered things.

Well, she'd wanted to know where her emotional attraction to Murad would lead and now she knew, she thought grimly. It had grown to the point where it was threatening to take over her entire life.

So, now what? She faced the question squarely. Should she cut and run or stay and face the consequences of having been stupid enough to have fallen in love with Murad?

Pain at the thought of never seeing him again cut through her uncertainty like a knife. She didn't have the willpower to leave him. Even though she was as certain as she could be that sooner or later he'd move on to other places and other women, she clung to the hope that it would be later. She wanted a little time to store up memories against a desolate future. Just because she knew her love was doomed didn't mean that she couldn't enjoy it now. And she would, she vowed. She had waited a long time to fall in love and she had the depressing feeling that she never would again. Compared to Murad, other men would pale to insignificance.

A feeling of peace washed over her at her decision. She was right. She knew she was. Love, even a one-sided love such as hers, was a rare commodity and deserved to be cherished. Her tense muscles slowly began to relax and she slipped into a deep, dreamless void of contentment.

A contentment that was rudely shattered several hours later by a series of indignant squeaks and yelps.

Eleanore rolled over and peered blearily at her bedside clock. It wasn't there. Groggily, she propped herself up on one elbow and looked around in confusion. Two things occurred to her simultaneously. She wasn't in her own bed and she wasn't wearing a nightgown. In fact, as she sat up in confusion, she realized she wasn't wearing anything at all.

Murad! Memory suddenly came rushing back. Her gaze swung to the other side of the king-size bed. Where was Murad? A slightly louder howl drove the question from her mind. Lacey was working herself up into a full-fledged protest. Obviously, the poor baby was starving. Eleanore glanced around, looking for her dress. She couldn't find it in the dim light spilling through the partially open sitting-room door, but she did find a long, white terry-cloth robe lying across the foot of the bed.

Hurriedly slipping into it, she belted its ample folds around her narrow waist and rushed into the sitting room, only to come to a precipitous halt at the sight that greeted her.

Murad was seated on the couch, wearing the twin to her white robe. Lacey was nestled in the crook of his left arm, and he was trying to convince the indignant baby to drink from the bottle he was holding. A warm surge of emotion went through her at the sight. It looked so right somehow. Murad and the tiny baby. He would make a wonderful father.

"How long has Lacey been up and what are you feeding her?" she asked in the hope of focusing his attention on the baby instead of what had happened between them earlier. She couldn't bear it if he were to attempt to rationalize their lovemaking. Or worse yet, she thought, swallowing against the sour taste of nausea, apologize. To her infinite relief, after one piercing look at her tense features, he followed her lead.

"Not long. She seemed hungry so I called room service and asked for a bottle, but I didn't know what brand of formula she eats so I guessed."

"I think you guessed wrong." She chuckled at the indignant expression on Lacey's tiny features. "Just a second while I get the emergency bottle in her bag." Eleanore hurried into the second bedroom, located the bottle, and was back a few seconds later.

"Poor little lamb." She scooped Lacey out of Murad's arms, trying not to notice the electricity that arced between them when her fingers brushed against his. At the rate she was becoming sensitized to him, in a few weeks all he'd have to do was to look at her and she'd dissolve into a steaming puddle of molten desire.

Snuggling Lacey into her arms, she sat down on one of the overstuffed chairs and popped the nipple into Lacey's mouth. The baby gave a snuffled snort and greedily began to guzzle the formula.

"Poor lamb, indeed," Murad agreed. "Having to drink that stuff." He set the rejected bottle on the coffee table. "Have you smelled it? Never mind tasting it." He leaned back into the couch's down-filled softness and propped his feet up on the coffee table.

His robe fell partially open at his movement, baring his legs to midthigh. Eleanore felt her mouth go dry as her eyes hungrily traced over the hard muscles rippling beneath a supple coating of tanned skin. Her stomach twisted in sudden longing as she remembered the abrasive feel of those legs pressed against her own.

"Have you tasted it?" he persisted.

No, but she'd truly tasted the fruits of love for the first time in her life, she thought dreamily as a flush warmed her pale skin. Hoping the room's dim light would disguise her reaction, she said, "Of course I haven't tasted it. But it's very nutritious."

"Not as nutritious as breast milk would be. Why didn't Kelly nurse her the way nature intended?"

"She tried, but . . ." Eleanore began, and then broke off as she realized exactly what he'd said.

"When did you find out about Kelly?" she whispered.

"When I had your background checked out," Murad admitted.

"You had no right to go snooping into my past." She decided that a good offense might really be the best defense.

"Possibly." His grudging admission surprised her. "But at the time I felt I was justified. Selim was clamoring to meet you and you were claiming not even to know who the father of your child was. What was I supposed to do? It seemed to me that you'd inherited a lot more from your mother than her beauty."

Her beauty? Eleanore savored his words. Murad really thought she was beautiful? Considering the women he normally associated with, that seemed highly unlikely. But it was equally unlikely that he'd lie to her. He might have a lamentable habit of omitting relevant facts, but she'd seen no evidence whatsoever that he would stoop to outright lying.

"My mother..." Eleanore instinctively sought to defend her and then paused as the full ramifications of what he'd said suddenly occurred to her. If he knew that Kelly was Lacey's mother then it was quite possible he knew where Kelly was. A rising sense of excitement filled her.

"Murad—" she leaned toward him "—do you know where Kelly is?"

"Kelly?" He shifted slightly and his robe parted still further, sending another wave of longing through her. Firmly squelching it, she persisted. "Quit stalling. Where is she?"

Murad studied her for a few minutes, his dark gaze sweeping thoughtfully over her eager face. Finally, he said, "I'm not going to tell you because much as it pains me to admit it, you have been right about your father."

"What?" Eleanore blinked in confusion. "What does my father have to do with my idiot cousin and her opting out of her responsibilities?"

"Everything from my point of view. Don't you see? It's exactly the same situation. I felt you had a responsibility to your father that you were refusing to meet."

"But—"

"Even admitting that he treated you badly, you still had a responsibility in my eyes. I felt you were dragging your feet, so I decided to force the issue by setting up this meeting. Now I'm not so sure that it wouldn't have been better in the long run to have waited until you felt secure enough to instigate the meeting yourself. It appears that all I managed to accomplish was to upset you to the point of tears." A look of regret tightened his features. "I knew you'd be angry, but I never thought . . ."

"I know." Eleanore grimaced. "You belong to the 'toss them into the pool' school of thought as opposed to the 'dunk one toe at a time.' But what does that have to do with Kelly's whereabouts?"

"Kelly left home to come to terms with her life."

"So she says," Eleanore replied.

"Well, just as hindsight has proved that I should have left you to make the first overture to Selim, maybe you should allow Kelly time to work out her own problems."

"But..." Eleanore spluttered in frustration. Of all the times for Murad to realize that he shouldn't meddle in other people's lives. She couldn't even derive much comfort from the fact that he not only had listened to her, but was willing to concede that she might have been right. "Listen, Murad, New York is a big city and Kelly is a singularly immature nineteen-year-old."

"Kelly is quite safe where she is," Murad assured her, "and Lacey is quite safe where *she* is. So why rock the boat?"

Because she was tired of rowing that boat, Eleanore admitted. Tired of being made a convenience of by her cousin. Tired of thinking up lies to tell her aunt about why Kelly didn't come to visit and most of all tired of not being free to live her own life. Even if that life had become hopelessly complicated by falling in love with Murad.

"You won't tell me?" she asked flatly.

"No, I won't tell you because I think you're right."

"Why do I find that such an empty comfort?"

"Because you're a woman and women are never satisfied?" The wicked glint in his eyes gave his teasing words a sensual connotation that sent her heart into overdrive. "And speaking of empty, Lacey's finished her bottle." Murad nodded at the baby.

"Oh, drat." She hastily yanked the collapsed nipple out of Lacey's pursed lips. Eleanore gently placed the baby against her shoulder and rubbed her back, hoping to bring the air up. She was successful. A series of belches shook the baby.

"That's a sweet little—" Eleanore frowned as a wet warmth dampened her robe. "What on earth?" She gingerly squeezed the baby's bottom and was rewarded by a damp squish. "She's soaking! Didn't you change her before you started to feed her?"

"I don't change diapers," Murad said placidly.

"But you were feeding her."

"Once the formula's in, it's no longer my responsibility. Men from my part of the world don't change diapers."

"Ha! Your part of the world, nothing. From what I've seen, men don't change diapers, period." Eleanore got to her feet, gingerly holding the sleepy baby away from her. "Tell me, would your sense of masculinity be threatened by carrying in her diaper bag?" She gestured toward the dark blue bag lying beside the couch where she had dropped it earlier.

"It isn't my masculinity that's threatened by diapers." He obligingly picked the bag up and trailed along behind her into the smaller bedroom. "It's my stomach."

"This is the same man who reduced a mugger to a gory mess with a few well-aimed blows?" She eyed him incredulously.

"There's gore and there's gore."

"Yeah." Eleanore deftly bundled the baby into a fresh diaper. "And there's logic and there's logic."

"Let me have her." Murad held his hands out once she had Lacey in a dry sleeper. "I'll hold her a second to make sure she's gotten rid of all the air."

"Thanks." Eleanore handed Lacey to him. "I need to take a shower."

She hurried into the bathroom off the larger bedroom and, rolling the dampened robe into a ball, shoved it into the clothes hamper.

She cast a longing glance at the huge bathtub. Much as she'd like a leisurely soak in it, she wanted to be back in bed before Murad returned. That way, if he didn't intend to continue their affair, he could sleep elsewhere. But if she waited until he was already in bed and climbed in with him only to find out that he regretted what had happened earlier, she'd die of embarrassment.

Hastily, she adjusted the water flow in the shower stall and stepped beneath its warm spray. Angling the water down to avoid wetting her hair, she picked up the soap and began to lather her body.

She hurriedly rinsed herself and, flipping off the water, reached for the towel she'd flung over the glass door. It wasn't there. She squinted, trying to see through the almost opaque glass. It must have fallen onto the floor. Muttering in frustration, Eleanore opened the door to look and found herself face-to-face with Murad.

A paralyzing wave of shyness gripped her as his eyes roamed over her dripping body. That was replaced by a sense of feminine power as she realize that Murad was as affected by her as she was by him. With a slow, seductive smile, she stepped into the large towel he held for her. He wrapped it around her and then swung her up into his arms and headed back into the bedroom.

"Lacey's asleep and you and I have the rest of the night." His brilliant, black eyes promised untold delights. "But you do realize that once we're back home we'll have to be absolutely circumspect, don't you? For the most part my household is from Abar. They hold to the old ways. If they thought we were lovers, you'd be typecast as a woman of loose morals, not deserving of or entitled to respect."

"That's archaic!"

"It may be archaic, but it's the way they think. You have to learn to deal with the world the way it is and not the way you want it to be. They—"

"It's all right. I understand." Eleanore stopped his words with a kiss. She couldn't bear to hear him put the limitations of their relationship into words. It would irrevocably cheapen what she felt. "But that's then. This is now." She slipped her hand into his robe and slowly rubbed the palm of her hand over his bare chest.

"Quite true." A slow, anticipatory smile curved his lips. "Now we have only ourselves to consider."

"Yes," Eleanore whispered, with no thought of denying her love the outlet it craved.

10

"THIS INVESTIGATION of yours is going nowhere fast, Murad." Eleanore closed the study door behind them and walked across the room. She leaned up against the arm of the leather chair he'd just sat down in and unbuckled her sandals. Kicking them off, she rubbed her aching arches.

Murad gently tugged on her arm, pulling her down across his lap.

Eleanore sighed longingly and snuggled against his chest, wishing he'd make love to her again.

"Feet hurt?" Murad misinterpreted her sigh. "You have absolutely no common sense when it comes to shoes."

"Maybe not, but I have great fashion sense." She sent a complacent look at her discarded sandals. "And I'm right about us having just wasted an entire evening. Consider it," she insisted when he frowned. "We spent...what?" She glanced at the antique clock on the mantel above the fireplace. "The last three hours socializing with that bunch of misfits from your office and what did we find out? That Walton still holds you in complete contempt and hates me. I could have told you that before we wasted the evening. Doesn't it bother you the way he treats you?" Eleanore remembered how her own blood had boiled at some of Walton's disparaging remarks to Murad. But Murad's assumed affability had remained unimpaired through it all.

"My turn will come." His face momentarily set in implacable lines and Eleanore shivered. Murad would make a frightening enemy. As she had no doubt Walton would find out if he didn't shape up. She just hoped she would still be here to see it.

A momentary sadness filled her at the thought of leaving, but she firmly suppressed it. She'd known from the beginning that this was a temporary arrangement; that she was living in a kind of make-believe world populated by characters straight out of the Arabian Nights.

She peered up into Murad's face and, encouraged by the feel of his hardening body beneath her hips, placed a kiss on the exact center of his chin. The rough-silk texture of his skin scraped across her soft lips, sending a jolt of desire through her.

"You taste like—" Her tongue darted out and traced over his lower lip. To her delight, he jerked as if he'd been struck.

"Like a man in the grip of an intolerable frustration?" he ground out. "And you aren't helping any."

"Oh dear." Eleanore leaned her head back against his shoulder and gave him a tantalizing smile. "And I did so want to be helpful. Perhaps if I were to try something else..." She deftly pulled off his tie, tossed it over her head and then proceeded to methodically unbutton his white shirt. Once she'd gotten it open, she buried her face in the cloud of crisp black hair on his chest and breathed deeply, filling her lungs with the warm, musky scent of his skin. Catching the hair between her lips, she tugged gently, smiling when he shuddered. She rubbed her palm over his chest, pausing to probe the beaded tip of one flat, masculine nipple.

Eleanore glanced up into his brilliant black eyes and the expression in them tightened the ache of desire throbbing in her abdomen.

"Tell me, Murad, just how much help do you need?" she asked provocatively.

"Where you're concerned, I'm beginning to think I'm helpless." He tilted her head up and fitted their mouths together, carefully molding the shape of her lips to his. The taste of him flooded her and, hungry for yet more contact, she opened her mouth.

His tongue boldly thrust inside, advancing and retreating in a parody of a greater intimacy, while his hand slipped the strap of her evening dress over her shoulder. He tugged the loose bodice down, baring her small breast.

"You're exquisite," he whispered as his hand covered her.

Eleanore whimpered as he rotated his palm over the peak, causing it to tighten into an aching nub of desire. The warmth of his fingers was like a brand on her creamy skin, heating her breast until it contracted to almost painful hardness.

Using the hard bar of his arm to arch her pliant body upward, his mouth closed hotly over her nipple, sucking strongly on it. Sharp splinters of sensation raced along her nerve endings, sending her senses spinning out of control. Eleanore gasped, feeling as if someone had cut off her oxygen supply, leaving her dizzy and disoriented.

Murad's hand slipped beneath her skirt, stroking over her thighs. When he reached the bare expanse of skin between the tops of her stockings and her briefs, he paused to knead the silky skin. Eleanore twisted against him, in the grip of an intolerable tension.

Gathering her against his chest, Murad stood up and, moving to his desk, set her down beside it. With fingers that trembled with the strength of his need, he yanked off her panties and, pushing her skirt up to her waist, lifted her onto the edge of the desktop. His eyes glittering, he moved between her legs and Eleanore's breath caught in an audible gasp as she felt the pulsating heat of his flesh boldly probing her vulnerable softness.

His mouth closed over hers at the same instant that he drove into her and he swallowed up her cry of shocked pleasure.

Frantically, she wrapped her legs around his waist and eagerly moved with him, meeting each of his hard thrusts as the pressure and tension coiling through her body inexorably tightened to a fever pitch.

"Murad!" She tore her mouth from his. "I can't stand this. I can't . . ." Her body suddenly went rigid as the tension shattered, showering her with a million tiny pinpricks of pleasure.

Murad pulled her head against his chest, muffling the sounds of her pleasure as, with a final thrust, he exploded within her.

For a long moment out of time, they simply clung together, too shaken by the depth of their reaction to move. Then, with a final shuddering breath, Murad gathered her up in his arms and sat back down on the leather chair.

"That magazine was right." Eleanore laughed weakly. "Men do find stockings and a garter belt sexier than panty hose."

"I don't know about men, but as far as I'm concerned, you'd look sexy in a gunnysack."

Eleanore snuggled closer, treasuring his compliment. She frowned in annoyance as the phone rang and Murad reached out to answer it. She resented anything that intruded on their all-too-rare moments alone.

"Good evening, Selim. Eleanore?" Murad glanced questioningly down at her.

She nodded and reached for the receiver. Precisely five minutes later her father said goodbye and hung up.

"That sounded amicable enough," Murad probed.

"It was. Actually—" she shivered as he slipped his hand beneath her deeply cut neckline and began to fondle her bare breast "—his having to leave for that OPEC meeting in Switzerland turned out to be a blessing in disguise."

"How so?"

"Because it means that I only have to worry about one thing at a time. When he was here, I had to deal with his physical presence as well as what he was saying. But this way, all I have to worry about is what he's saying and, since we agreed to limit our phone calls to just five minutes every night, they aren't so long that I run out of things to talk about."

"It sounds as if you're reaching some kind of understanding with him."

"After a fashion. It'd probably be more accurate to say that we're laying the groundwork for a better understanding. When he returns to New York in a few weeks, we should be able to spend some time together without either of us feeling that we have to fake an emotion we don't feel."

Murad sighed. "I wish I were having as much success with my problem. Unfortunately, you're right about this evening, Eleanore. We didn't learn one damn thing that we didn't already know. There has to be something I'm missing." His voice was laced with frustration.

"Maybe, but for the life of me I don't see what. Of course, I'm not a spy, but—"

"Information gatherer."

"Whatever." She shrugged, shivering as the movement caused her breast to scrape across his palm. "What will you do if you can't figure out who's responsible?"

"Get rid of the whole office and start from scratch. And I'd hate to do that because there's no way I could keep the reason quiet."

"And the knowledge would irrevocably damage all their reputations, which would hardly be fair to the innocent," Eleanore pointed out.

"I hope it won't come to that. But whatever comes, it's going to have to come swiftly. I can't take many more evenings like this one."

"You could always bring Sonia along to liven things up." Even though she knew that Murad had only used Sonia as a prop in his masquerade, her curiosity about the woman ran rampant. It seemed inconceivable to her that a man could be around a woman that beautiful and that willing and not eventually fall under her spell.

"I sent her out to L.A. for a screen test last week as her final payoff. We'll have to write her out of our script." The casual lack of interest in his voice warmed

Eleanore's heart. That was one less thing she had to worry about.

"I—" He broke off as the phone rang again. He picked it up, listened a moment and then answered in Arabic.

"I'll see you in the morning, Murad." Eleanore got to her feet and straightened her clothing before leaving the room. She wanted to give him privacy for his call. She didn't want him to think she was trying to take over his life. Besides, she thought as she made her way upstairs, she really was tired. She'd spent far too many nights lately lying awake, worrying about their relationship. What she needed was a good night's sleep.

RATHER TO HER SURPRISE, she not only got a good night's sleep, but it extended well into the next morning. Appalled at how late it was when she finally awoke, she'd hurried into her clothes and rushed down to the breakfast room only to be told by Wilkerson that Murad had left the house almost an hour before.

The sympathy on Wilkerson's face at her disappointment pulled her up short. Was her love for Murad so obvious? She sincerely hoped not. She had more pride than to wear her heart on her sleeve for everyone to see.

"Would you care for breakfast, Miss Eleanore?" Wilkerson asked solicitously.

"I'll just have some coffee." She poured herself a cup from the pot sitting on the Chinese Chippendale sideboard. She'd wasted far too much time this past week mooning over Murad, she told herself. It was time she remembered her primary goal, finding Kelly. Thoughtfully, she began to sip her coffee. So far, her attempts to find her cousin had been singularly unsuccessful. She'd briefly considered doing as Murad had suggested and wait for Kelly to come to her senses and return home. Unfortunately, knowing her cousin, that might take years.

"I must say, living in the lap of luxury doesn't seem to have done you much good," Liz's astringent voice broke into Eleanore's frustrated thoughts.

"Liz!"

"The young woman says she's a friend of yours, Miss Eleanore." Wilkerson hovered protectively in the doorway.

"My oldest." Eleanore grinned happily at Liz, glad to see her. "Get yourself a cup of coffee and tell me to what I owe the pleasure."

"No coffee, thanks." Liz furtively watched as Wilkerson withdrew and then demanded, "Is he real? I thought characters like that only existed in moviemakers' imaginations."

"Or on Murad's payroll," Eleanore said. "You wouldn't believe his staff. He's got a French chef in the kitchen who doesn't cook, he creates. He even has a gardener for the houseplants."

"Lucky you."

"Even the Garden of Eden had its serpent," Eleanore muttered.

"Does it have something to do with this?" Liz handed her the newspaper she was carrying.

Eleanore read the headline, "Playboy Prince's Latest Playmate," her eyes widening in dismay as she realized the picture splashed across the front page was of her and Murad.

"Damn!" she muttered. "I sure hope Aunt Theresa doesn't see this."

"That's all you've got to say?" Liz demanded.

"Come on, Liz. You know what these scandal sheets are like. That picture must have been taken earlier in the week when we were entertaining some of his colleagues at a restaurant. There were eight other people at that table. The newspaper simply blacked them out of the photo.

"Well, then, let's discuss Lacey. Where's my favorite baby?"

"In the nursery with her nanny."

"Nanny!" Liz yelped. "You've got a nanny?"

"No, Lacey has a nanny." Eleanore grinned.

"Let me guess? A first cousin to Mary Poppins?"

"Gloria Steinem might be closer." Eleanore chuckled. "Murad got her as a stopgap from the French ambassador to the U.N."

"I take it that means you haven't found Kelly yet?"

"No, every avenue I try ends up a dead end. She hasn't shown up at the university for classes, she hasn't contacted her mother..."

"What about her friends?"

"I have a feeling about one of them," Eleanore said slowly. "Remember Barbra Majoric? Well, I've been calling her every couple of days and the last time I talked to her she was different somehow."

"Barbra Majoric is different, full stop," Liz said scathingly. "That girl would keep a team of psychiatrists busy for a lifetime."

"She'll outgrow it." Eleanore shrugged.

"Sure, and the world may outgrow war, but I'm not holding my breath in the meantime."

"At any rate," Eleanore continued, "I'd be willing to bet Kelly's been in touch with her, but she denies it."

"Frustrating, but not surprising." Liz shrugged. "And there's not much we can do about it, since most professionals frown on thumbscrews."

"Pity," Eleanore said, "sometimes the old ways are the best."

"My sentiments exactly." Wilkerson spoke from the doorway. "Have you considered bribing this Barbra? Or are you morally opposed to it?"

"It isn't scruples that are stopping me," Eleanore said gloomily. "It's money. I can't spare enough to make it worth her while to tell me anything."

"How much might that be?" Wilkerson persisted.

"Oh, she'd probably sing for a couple of hundred."

"Then that's no problem." Wilkerson beamed at her. "Ali left several thousand dollars with me when he had to return to Abar. He said it was to be used for emergencies, and this certainly sounds like an emergency. Just a moment while I get the funds."

"My God!" Liz watched him hurry away. "Where on earth did Murad get him from? Ian Fleming?"

"Fleming's dead," Eleanore muttered absently, wondering if it was ethical to use Murad's money to find Kelly, when Murad already knew where Kelly was.

"Which is what we're going to be when your Arabic friend finds out he's funding a spot of bribery."

"You've got to be kidding," Eleanore scoffed. "I shudder to think what he's funded in his day."

"Yeah." Liz grinned. "I remember the pictures of him and the blonde."

Eleanore made no attempt to correct Liz's erroneous assessment of Murad. It would involve too many explanations, some of which weren't hers to make.

"Here you are, Miss Eleanore." Wilkerson handed her a plain white vellum envelope. "Good luck."

"Thanks." Eleanore smiled at him. "We're going to need it. Come on, Liz, let's get this over with."

CONTRARY TO ELEANORE'S FEARS, bribing Barbra turned out to be relatively easy. After a few token denials, she'd quickly capitulated at the sight of the money Eleanore pulled out of her purse. Although she'd claimed that she didn't know where Kelly was living, she had given them the name and address of the place where she said Kelly was working.

"This is it, ladies." The taxi driver gave them a dubious look as he pulled up in front of a run-down building near Times Square.

"Thank you." Eleanore paid him, and giving the equally dubious-looking Liz a poke, climbed out of the cab.

"Good Lord!" Eleanore averted her eyes from the explicit magazine covers plastered all over the store's front window.

"What'd you expect from a place called Aphrodite's Delight?" Liz asked.

"Aphrodite was a temptress. This stuff isn't a temptation. It's a full-fledged assault," Eleanore said in distaste.

"And it may be a wild-goose chase," Liz pointed out.

"I know. But as long as we're here, we might as well go inside and see if Kelly really does work here."

"I guess." Liz reluctantly followed Eleanore into the store. Once inside, Eleanore stopped, giving her eyes time to adjust to the dim lighting. She wrinkled her nose at the smell of sour wine—mixed with other less appetizing aromas—that hung like a blanket over the crowded shelves.

Glancing around, she saw a large sign hanging from the ceiling near the back of the store with the word Cashier printed on it in phosphorescent yellow paint. She pointed to it. "Let's ask about Kelly there." She started down a narrow aisle, only to come to a precipitous halt as her eyes lit on something to her left.

"I was wrong," she muttered. "They *do* make them."

"Make what?" Liz asked with a wary look over her shoulder at a disreputable-looking young man who was sitting on the floor, staring in glassy-eyed wonder at the ceiling fan's slow revolutions.

"Silver orthopedic shoes." Eleanore picked up a square-heeled, lace-up, silver-lamé oxford. "Except for the color they look like something an octogenarian would wear. That and all the rhinestones." She eyed the profusion of glittering stones covering the low heel with distaste. "Why anyone would want these is beyond me."

Liz grabbed the shoe out of Eleanore's hand and shoved it back on the shelf. "That's because you haven't got a foot fetish! For heaven's sake, keep moving. I don't like the looks of that character behind us."

"Foot fetish?" Eleanore stared more closely at the silver shoes. "What do you know about foot fetishes?"

"Apparently more than you do," Liz said with a nervous glance over her shoulder. The glassy-eyed young man was attempting to stand up. "I studied the subject in a class on deviant sexual behavior. Now forget the shoes and move."

"I'm going." Eleanore took a deep breath, immediately regretting the action when her stomach rolled protestingly. Ignoring it, she hurried toward the sign.

Liz was right. This wasn't the time or the place to indulge in idle curiosity.

Eleanore eyed the man behind the counter with surprise. His clothes looked like a casual version of *Dress
for Success*. He most definitely didn't reflect his surroundings.

"May I help you, ladies?" He seemed as surprised to
see them as they were to see him.

"I hope so." Eleanore gave him what she hoped was
a conspiratorial smile. "I'm looking for Kelly."

"Kelly?" he repeated thoughtfully. "Sorry, ladies,
that's a new one on me. Where'd you hear about Kelly?"

"Barbra gave us this address," Eleanore replied,
hoping the mention of Barbra would make him more
forthcoming. Unfortunately, there was still the very real
possibility that Barbra had lied to them and this man
really didn't know about Kelly. Or, perhaps, he was
simply waiting for them to make it worth his while to
tell them.

Stifling a sigh, Eleanore yanked out the remainder of
the roll of bills Wilkerson had given her. "If it's a question of money—"

"You're new at this, aren't you, sweetheart? Let me
give you a tip. Never flash a wad that size in a place like
this. We've got customers who'd slit your throat for the
price of a fix."

"Yeah." Liz glanced over her shoulder at the young
man who was now propped up against the shelves at
the end of the aisle, leering at them. "We've already met
one."

"Thanks for the advice," Eleanore said impatiently,
"but what about Kelly?"

"Freeze right where you are! This is a drug raid!" The bullhorn-amplified voice bounced off the walls.

ALMOST TWO HOURS LATER Daugherty, the cop who had arrested them and then left them to cool their heels in the crowded squad room, returned.

"You're each entitled to a phone call," he snapped. "You can use the phone over there." He nodded to the desk behind them and then left.

"Do you know the name of a good lawyer?" Liz asked Eleanore.

"I don't even know the name of a bad one. I'm going to try Murad."

"Think he'll come?" Liz asked.

"What I'm hoping is that he'll call someone to arrange bail."

Liz shrugged. "It's worth a try. He can only say no."

Ha! Eleanore thought. Murad could, and probably would, say a whole lot more. But as long as he said it after he rescued them, she didn't care.

Taking a deep breath, she dialed Murad's office number.

"Ahiqar here." His deep voice flowed soothingly over her frazzled nerves.

"Murad, this is Eleanore. I...um...that is..." she stammered, trying to find the right words to explain her predicament.

"Yes?" he said encouragingly, his voice warm. "What's the problem?"

"Nothing much...except...except that Liz and I have been arrested and we need the name of a good lawyer," she finally blurted out.

"Arrested!" Murad bellowed.

She switched the receiver to the other ear and said, "Don't shout into the phone."

"You must forgive my surprise," he said sarcastically, "but I found the news a bit of a shock."

"Well, it wasn't a picnic for us either," she shot back.

"Exactly what are the charges against you?"

"I'm not positive, but I think it's a morals charge."

"What?"

"I told you not to yell into the phone. And it's all your fault anyway."

"My fault!"

"Yes, yours," she insisted. "If you'd just have told me where Kelly was, I wouldn't have been in that sex store trying to buy information. You know, Murad, they really do sell silver orthopedic shoes."

"Quit trying to change the subject," he said. "Just tell me where you are."

"The Twelfth Precinct station house."

"I'll be right there." He slammed down the receiver.

"Well?" Liz demanded impatiently when Eleanore rejoined her. "What'd he say?"

"He'll be right over."

"Good."

"I hope you still think so after he gets here," Eleanore said dubiously. "He didn't sound any too happy about the situation."

"In all fairness, would you like it if your houseguest called and asked to be bailed out? And on a morals charge, yet? Maybe he'll cool off on the ride over," Liz offered hopefully.

He hadn't, Eleanore realized when, fifteen minutes later, she watched him stalk across the long squad room, flanked by four gray-suited men.

"The cavalry has arrived." Liz got to her feet.

Murad stopped directly in front of Eleanore, his dark eyes raking over her pale face. "Are you all right?" He reached out and ran his forefinger across her cheek, his gentle caress at odds with his severe expression.

"I'm okay," she said huskily.

He turned to Liz. "And you, Dr. Lawton?"

"If you discount furious, I'm fine, too. I—"

Daugherty caught sight of them and hurried across the bustling room. "Stay away from the prisoners."

"Prisoners?" Murad bit the word off, shattering it into icy shards.

"What have you charged these two young women with?" the distinguished elderly man to Murad's right asked. "When we attempted to pay their bail tickets at the front desk we were told they hadn't as yet been charged."

"I haven't decided whether I'm going to charge them or not," Daugherty muttered.

"Then on what grounds are you detaining them?" the man continued relentlessly.

"They were in a store that sells sexually explicit material," Daugherty blustered.

"Which is not a crime in New York City," the elderly man pointed out.

"She had a wad of bills in her hand and she wasn't the least bit cooperative."

"The next time you want cooperation don't wave a shotgun in someone's face," Eleanore snapped.

"He threatened you?" Murad's voice was menacing and Daugherty instinctively backed up a step.

Murad reached out and encircled Eleanore's slender shoulders and pulled her up against his body.

For a second, Eleanore allowed herself the luxury of sagging against him, of drawing support from his strength. In his arms, she felt more than capable of handling a dozen Daughertys.

"Now, just a minute here," Daugherty blustered. "I'm the cop."

"And, as such, you should be aware of the law," the elderly man observed dispassionately.

"If you have grounds to arrest them, do so." Murad eyed Daugherty coldly.

"Oh, hell, just forget it." Daugherty shrugged.

"No," Murad purred. "I will not forget your pointing a gun at Eleanore. My lawyers will be filing a formal complaint with the Commissioner's office."

"Now, see here . . ." Daugherty began to look worried.

"I have already seen more than enough of you," Murad snapped. "James," he addressed one of the men with him, "please see that Dr. Lawton gets home. I'll take care of Miss Fulton."

Liz gave Eleanore a sympathetic look. "Give me a call later," she said as she left with the young lawyer Murad had spoken to.

Providing I'm allowed phone calls, Eleanore thought ruefully as Murad shepherded her out of the building with the remaining three men flanking them like an honor guard. Murad might have supported her in front of Daugherty, but what he would have to say in private was another matter entirely. She had felt the tension tightening his body when she'd leaned against him and she was relatively certain it was caused by suppressed anger.

She sighed in despair. She loved Murad so much. And she wanted the time they had together to be special. So what had she done? Involved him in an unsavory mess.

"We'll take a cab back to our office, Your Excellency," the elderly man said. "And I'll file a complaint with the Commissioner's office this afternoon. Do you wish to sue, Miss Fulton?"

"No. I simply want to make sure that nitwit is forced to think twice before he waves a shotgun at anyone again. One of these days he's going to kill somebody accidentally."

"It won't be you." Murad's words had the ring of a vow. "Thank you for your prompt response, gentlemen." He shook their hands and then opened the door of the Rolls that had pulled up beside them.

Eleanore climbed into the back seat of the car and Murad followed her, slamming the door behind him. He barked out a command to the driver in Arabic and then leaned back against the seat as the Rolls pulled into traffic.

Beginning to get angry, Eleanore frowned at the unyielding expression on his face. It wasn't as if she'd committed a crime or something; she'd simply been the victim of circumstances.

"I'm sorry you were inconvenienced," she said stiffly, "but I don't think—"

"That much is glaringly obvious!"

Eleanore clamped her lips together and turned to stare out the window. If he wanted to wallow in self-righteous anger, let him. She'd offered an apology for something that hadn't even been her fault. That was as far as she was willing to go to placate him.

She was still staring blindly out the window when the driver pulled up in front of a glass and concrete high rise. Murad motioned Eleanore out of the car, said something in Arabic to the driver and then hustled her into the building.

With a nod to the guard at the reception desk, Murad steered her through the lobby of what appeared to be a very expensive apartment house. Eleanore swallowed uneasily. Had her brush with the law today convinced Murad that she was an undesirable houseguest? Had he decided to move her out of his house and into the anonymity of an apartment complex?

She stole a worried look at his taut face as the elevator silently sped upward. He certainly looked angry enough to do it. She grimaced, wishing he'd calm down long enough to listen to her explanation.

The elevator came to a silent stop on the thirty-second floor and Murad took her arm and marched her down the thickly carpeted hallway. She felt exactly like an unruly toddler being yanked along by an irate adult.

Murad unlocked the door of apartment 32F, pushed her inside and slammed the door behind them.

Suddenly, without warning, he grabbed her arm and yanked her toward him. Taken off balance, she sprawled against his chest.

His arms closed around her like a vise and his lips met hers with bruising force. There was no gentleness or finesse behind his kiss. It was motivated by sheer masculine need. His mouth pressed against hers, forcing it open to admit his thrusting tongue.

A star-burst of excitement exploded in her mind, its brilliance dissolving her instinctive resistance to such overwhelming aggression.

Murad's fingers speared through her hair, dislodging the pins holding her chignon and the silky strands tumbled over his hand. He held her head still as his mouth plundered hers with devastating thoroughness.

Eleanore's fingers clutched at his suit jacket, seeking a stable anchor in the storm of passion he'd so suddenly unleashed. This kiss was entirely different from the others they'd shared. She felt as if she were on a runaway roller coaster with no other option but to hang on to the end.

Finally, he released her and, leaning his forehead against hers, said slowly, "Eleanore, you'll be the death of me yet."

"Oh?"

"Yes, 'oh.'" He swung her up in his arms and carried her across the large living room. "You're harder to keep track of than a whole damn spy ring."

"It's a talent." She chuckled, feeling incredibly light-hearted now that she knew his reaction had been caused by fear and not anger. "Where are we?" she asked as he walked through an open doorway and into a huge bedroom decorated in neutral beiges.

"Your father's apartment. He leased it last month while he was waiting for you to make up your mind about seeing him. He gave me the key to keep an eye on things when he went to Switzerland."

"How convenient." Eleanore gave him a slow smile as she suddenly realized why he'd brought her here.

"I couldn't agree more." He dropped her onto the bed and began to strip off his clothes. "Living with you, but having to hide behind closed doors if I want to touch you, is slowly driving me insane."

Eleanore watched as he unzipped his pants and stepped deftly out of them, her eyes focusing helplessly on his swollen manhood. She could feel the blood quickening in her veins, making her breasts tighten and ache with desire. A remembered tension began to build between her thighs and a small sound of longing bubbled out of her throat.

She wanted him, wanted him with a primitive intensity that had no basis in logic or reason. It was as if each time they made love she became more addicted to his touch. Under normal circumstances, she would have found the knowledge extremely disquieting, but now all she could think about was Murad. The taste of him, the feel of him deep within her. Nothing else mattered. Not the future. Not the past. Not who he was or what he owned. The only important thing was that she loved him—and she wanted to express that love in the most basic way possible.

Murad dropped onto the bed beside her, his features sharp with the passion seething through him. Hastily, he unbuttoned her shirt, pushed aside her bra and then pulled off her jeans.

Capturing her mouth, he boldly thrust his tongue inside. Her response was as instantaneous as if a match had been put to tinder. She feverishly pressed against him, feeling the rough texture of his body hair scraping across her soft skin, and her desire suddenly spiraled out of control. She was on fire for him. All the anxiety of her impossible morning suddenly found an outlet in Murad. Boldly she imitated his actions with her tongue.

It seemed to inflame him. He quickly moved between her thighs and positioned himself.

Eleanore whimpered longingly at the feel of his heated flesh and then gasped as he took her with one sure surge.

"Murad!" His name came out as a keening cry. She wrapped her legs around his hips and eagerly met each of his hard thrusts. She closed her eyes, her mind turned inward, focused on the escalating tension tightening her body.

He grasped her hips and raised her more fully into his deep sensual strokes, intensifying the feeling almost past bearing. She felt as if she would die in agony if he were to stop, and then suddenly she thought she would die anyway as his quickening rhythm finally snapped the cord tethering her to earth and she was whirled away into a vortex of pleasure so intense she felt faint.

"That's my darling." Murad's harsh voice encouraged her as he increased his own movements. Suddenly, he stiffened, the cords on his neck standing out against his bronzed skin as his own pleasure overtook him and he collapsed on her.

Eleanore slowly surfaced through layer upon layer of satiety to become aware of Murad's limp body sprawled across hers. Lovingly, she ran her fingertips down over his spine, smiling as a small shudder shook his seemingly boneless body. She loved him so much.

"I'm sorry," he murmured. "I was on you like a rutting bull. But, when you add the trauma of hauling you out of that police station to my general level of frustration—" He rolled onto his side and gathered her up in his arms. "I was so worried and furious with you for putting yourself in a position to be threatened by some idiot with a shotgun . . ."

He shrugged and Eleanore shivered at the movement of his body against hers. "The unvarnished truth is that the minute I touched you I went up in flames."

"You aren't the only one." She wiggled voluptuously. "If it's any comfort to you, I wasn't too happy about the situation I found myself in, either. Believe me, next time I'll be more cautious."

"There won't be a next time," he said flatly. "I still think you had a good point when you said people should be allowed to work out their problems, but frankly, I'm more concerned about stopping you from roaming the streets of New York than I am about Kelly's emerging psyche."

"You'll tell me where she is?" Eleanore asked hopefully.

"I'll take you myself. Just as soon as the driver gets back."

"When will that be?"

"I told him to return in two hours, which leaves us—" he raised his wrist and checked the time "—an hour and forty-seven minutes."

"Well . . ." Eleanore smiled into his night-dark eyes. "Since we've probably just set the record for the quickest bout of lovemaking, would you care to try for something a little longer?"

"You have the best ideas." He reached for her with an approving smile.

11

A SMALL EXCLAMATION of disappointment escaped Eleanore as the Rolls pulled into the parking lot beside a familiar apartment house. So much for the efficiency of Murad's spy network.

"This is Barbra Majoric's address," she said to Murad.

"And undoubtedly quite a few other people's, considering its size," Murad returned. "But it also happens to be the location of apartment 6-C, belonging to one David Tyler, a graduate student at Columbia with whom Kelly is living."

"Lacey's father?"

Murad shrugged. "I didn't request that information, but it seems likely."

"I see," she said slowly. Then, eager to get the coming confrontation over with, she reached for the door handle.

"Eleanore?" Murad covered her hand with his.

Eleanore trembled slightly, not entirely able to suppress her instinctive reaction. She stared down at his lean, brown fingers wondering what it was about this particular man's touch that made her senses leap. It wasn't as if he were spectacularly handsome or fantastically built. And it certainly wasn't because he catered to her every whim.

"If I may have your attention?" His tone was indulgent.

"Sorry. I was just trying to decide how to approach Kelly," she lied.

"If you take my advice you won't approach her at all. You'll let Kelly work out her own problems."

"But it isn't just Kelly's problem. It's also Lacey's. Who's looking out for her interests?"

"You are, and doing a much better job of it than Kelly could ever hope to do. Is it that you don't want the responsibility? Is that why you're so determined to find Kelly?"

"No, of course not. I love Lacey." Eleanore's voice cracked from the intensity of her feelings. "If I were the only one to be considered, I'd take Lacey in a flash. But don't you see? I'm not. Believe me, I know what it's like when a child is left with relatives, even loving relatives. I spent my childhood weaving impossible dreams about someday being able to live with my mother. I never really enjoyed what I did have because I was too busy wishing for what I didn't have."

Murad's hand tightened comfortingly over hers.

"I want something better for Lacey. I want her to have her own mother."

"And if Kelly refuses? Then what?"

"It won't come to that," Eleanore tried to sound positive. "I know Kelly loves her."

"But what if she loves this David Tyler she's living with more?"

It was a fear Eleanore shared. Once she would have scoffed at the idea that a loving mother could abandon her child for a man, but now, loving Murad as she did, she could understand the forces that might be driving her cousin. Understand and sympathize, even if she couldn't condone Kelly's actions.

"I'll cross that bridge if and when I come to it," she said.

"Well, if you're determined to do it, let's go." Murad leaned across her and opened the car door.

Eleanore took a deep breath of the tangy cologne that clung to him, drawing it deep into her lungs. It helped to bolster her courage.

"Murad, I don't mean to be unreasonable and I know I would never have found Kelly myself, but . . ."

"But you want to confront her on your own?" His dark eyes narrowed.

"Yes. You don't mind, do you?"

"Actually, I do. But I also understand what you're trying to say. Go ahead, Eleanore. I'll wait here for you."

"I won't be long." She smiled gratefully at him.

"It doesn't matter. I'll wait."

Eleanore studied his watchful eyes, sensing hidden meanings beneath his prosaic words. Telling herself she was being fanciful, she stepped out of the Rolls and headed toward the apartment building.

She had no trouble locating apartment 6-C. She paused for a moment outside the door to gather her thoughts and then rang the bell. The door was opened almost immediately by Kelly, whose face fell ludicrously at the sight of her cousin.

"That was my reaction when you disappeared." Eleanore took advantage of Kelly's surprise to walk into the apartment. Curiously, she glanced around the one-room efficiency. She could understand why Kelly hadn't taken Lacey with her. Two adults and a baby would be a very tight squeeze in these quarters.

"I can't talk to you now," Kelly whispered with a furtive glance at the half-open door in the far wall. "I'll meet you later at—"

"No." Eleanore shook her head. "We'll talk now. I've had enough of chasing you all over New York."

"Then why did you?" Kelly asked sullenly.

"Certainly not for the pleasure of your company," Eleanore snapped. "It concerns your daughter, remember? The one you left with Mrs. Benton."

"What daughter?" a stocky young man demanded from the now open door in the far wall.

David Tyler? Eleanore wondered, waiting for Kelly to answer him. When she didn't, Eleanore said, "Lacey Danielle, born July second of this year."

"What?" His swarthy skin seemed to drain of color. Even his lips went white. "My Lord," he muttered and slumped down on a dilapidated armchair. "I have a child?" He seemed to have trouble comprehending the fact.

"David . . ." Kelly began tentatively.

"Why didn't you tell me?" he demanded.

"I didn't mean to get pregnant."

"Well that makes us even because I didn't mean to get you pregnant. But that still doesn't tell me why you didn't bother to inform me I was going to be a father."

"But when I found out I was pregnant, I asked you if you wanted to get married and you said we didn't have the money until you'd completed your medical degree."

"And it didn't occur to you that mentioning we were going to be parents might alter the situation?"

"I don't see how," Kelly defended herself. "I mean we haven't got any more money just because we've got Lacey."

"We may not have any more money, but we sure as hell have a lot more responsibility." He raked his fingers through his shaggy black hair.

"I was going to tell you," Kelly insisted. "I was just waiting for the right moment. Oh, David, it's all so confusing." She began to sob.

"No, love, it isn't the least bit confusing." He took a deep breath and tried for a grin that didn't quite come off. "It's very simple. We have a daughter and she should be living with us, not—" He glanced at the silently listening Eleanore.

"My cousin, Eleanore," Kelly muttered. "But what about your dream of being a doctor? I don't want to spoil that for you." She sobbed all the harder.

"Don't, love." David put his arms around her. "It's not the end of the world. I have a bachelor's degree in chemistry. I can easily get a job as a lab technician."

"Am I right in assuming that you already have the funding lined up to pay for your medical degree?" Eleanore asked.

"Yes, providing I only eat two meals a day and don't buy anything frivolous like dental care or clothes," he said wryly.

"Then if you're taken care of—"

"I'm not the problem. My daughter is. Babies need good, nutritious food and health care and shoes and toys."

"I told Kelly I'd provide for her and Lacey while she was going to college. I'm still willing to do it whether she lives with me or with you."

"Thank you, but I can provide for my family without charity," he said stiffly.

Eleanore hurried to placate his pride. "I'm not offering you charity. I'm offering you a loan because I love my cousin and little Lacey. It seems to me that you and Kelly will have a much happier marriage if it's not filled with might-have-beens."

"I'd never blame Kelly!"

"But I'd blame myself," Kelly insisted. "I'd always feel guilty. And you'd make such a great doctor, David."

"And a doctor is going to be much more able to provide for Lacey financially than a lab technician," Eleanore pointed out. "And when all's said and done, Kelly and Lacey are my family and families stick together."

"Someday I'll introduce you to mine and you can see the fallacy of that particular argument," David said.

"Please, David," Kelly begged.

"All right," he agreed, capitulating, "but only on the condition that it really is a loan."

"Agreed." Eleanore nodded.

"And I can baby-sit for people to help our finances," Kelly happily put in. "The message board down in the laundry room is filled with people needing sitters. Now that I'm going to be your wife I won't need to train for anything."

Eleanore bit back her instinctive protest. She'd seen far too many marriages break up, leaving the homemaker suddenly thrust into the labor force with no marketable skills, to ever agree with Kelly's naive judgment. But she'd already interfered enough. The important thing was that Lacey would be safe. She'd grow up secure in the knowledge of who she was and where she belonged. And if Kelly was making a mistake by foregoing her education, it was her mistake to make.

"When can I get Lacey, Eleanore?" Kelly asked eagerly. "I want to show her to David."

"How about if I bring her and her paraphernalia by tomorrow morning?" Eleanore suggested.

"Fine," David agreed. "That'll give us time to clean out the dressing room and scrub down the walls. It'll make a nice nursery."

"It'd better." Kelly giggled. "It's the only spare space we've got. Would you like a cup of coffee, Eleanore?"

"No, thanks. I left a friend waiting downstairs. I'll see you tomorrow, first thing."

"WELL?" Murad demanded as she climbed back into the Rolls.

"Kelly may be immature, but she can certainly pick men. David Tyler took the news of his daughter's existence a whole lot better than anyone had a right to expect."

"He wants Lacey?"

"Yes. He was all set to give up his medical studies and get a job."

"At which point you offered to pay for Kelly and Lacey?"

"Why do you say that?" she asked curiously.

"I know you. You're a pushover where your family's concerned."

"Well, I'd already promised to support them while Kelly was in school. At least this way they'll be happy," Eleanore explained. "I promised to deliver Lacey to them tomorrow morning. Do you mind if I borrow a car to help move her stuff?"

"Of course not. Are you giving them Miss Kelvington, too? Her salary's already been paid through the end of the year."

Eleanore looked at Murad, a gleam of amusement brightening her eyes. "I'd love to sic Miss Kelvington on Kelly. She'd soon shape her up. But in the interest of David's sanity, I'd better not."

"A vindictive woman is a terrible thing." Murad chuckled. "Remind me never to cross you."

"Ha! You've been thwarting me since the day we met."

"But with the best of intentions."

"You know what they say about the road to hell being paved with good intentions."

"Not in my culture."

"But what is your culture?" Her intense curiosity about him got the better of her and she risked probing.

Murad grimaced. "Sometimes I wonder myself. My roots are eastern, but my outlook is strictly western. Much as I love Abar, I could never live there on a permanent basis. The way of life is far too restrictive."

"I see." Eleanore glanced down to hide the relief in her eyes. So Murad wasn't planning on returning to the Middle East.

But her relief was short-lived when she realized that there was no longer any real reason for her to continue to live with Murad, other than the fact that she loved him to distraction. Without the cost of Lacey's day care, she would have no trouble making ends meet on her salary as a substitute teacher. And from Murad's point of view he'd already accomplished what he'd set out to do when he'd first asked her to be his houseguest. She'd met her father and served as his hostess, although she'd been singularly unsuccessful in helping to catch the thief.

He might actually be relieved to have his home to himself again. And she was only moving across town, she thought, trying to raise her plummeting spirits. He could easily come to see her any time he wanted to.

Taking a deep breath, she said, "Now that I've found Kelly, there's no reason for me to continue to impose on your hospitality. I can move my things out at the same time I deliver Lacey."

"We had a deal, Eleanore Fulton!" His face hardened. "You were to help me in exchange for my helping you. Yet now that you no longer need my help, you intend to conveniently forget the rest of it?"

She peered uncertainly at him, surprised by his emphatic reaction. "But I thought you'd like having your house to yourself again."

"It may have escaped your notice, but I already share my home with quite a few people. You, to paraphrase a friend, are the pick of the litter."

"What an elegant turn of phrase you have, my dear sir." Eleanore laughed from the sheer pleasure of knowing that Murad wanted her to stay close to him. The heady knowledge bubbled through her like champagne. "When I consider that you prefer me to the epitome of an English butler, I'm overwhelmed."

"You should be," Murad said promptly. "Wilkerson is an original. I had to get my father to order our ambassador to London to let me borrow him."

"I don't think you should give him back," Eleanore said seriously. "He's the perfect butler for a spy. He was right there with the money for the bribe when I couldn't figure out how to handle Barbra."

"I wish he'd been there with a key to lock you up till you came to your senses," Murad grumbled.

"Maybe you ought to discuss your thief with him," Eleanore suggested jokingly.

"That's the only thing I haven't tried. There has to be something I'm missing, but what?" Murad clenched his fist in frustration.

"How much money would it have taken to have bought the first piece of property?" Eleanore asked, thinking that, perhaps, they could look for someone who had come into a large sum of money at about that time.

"Unfortunately, not that much. You don't really have to buy the property. You can simply buy an option on it. And the amount needed to purchase the option would have been well within the range of anyone in the office."

"Scotch that theory," Eleanore said regretfully. "How about lie-detector tests?"

"No." Murad shook his head. "For two reasons. It would irrevocably damage my relationship with the innocent staff and, more importantly, lie detectors aren't all that accurate. They have a horrendous margin of error, particularly if the subject is nervous."

"We can always fall back on yet another social event. Only this time let's have it at the office," she said slowly.

"Why there?"

"To put them on their own turf, so to speak. Maybe they'd feel less on guard in familiar surroundings."

"Could be." Murad frowned thoughtfully at the passing cars. "I noticed several of the people I tried to talk to at the last party at the house seemed distinctly ill at ease."

"They were probably afraid of spilling the punch on that gorgeous oriental carpet in the front living room. I know I was."

"It's too late to worry about it now. People have been spilling things on it for over a thousand years."

"A thousand years!" Eleanore gasped. "You walk on something that old!"

"Of course I walk on it. What else would I do with it? It's much too big to hang on a wall."

"You should . . ." she began and then subsided at his genuinely puzzled look. It seemed to Eleanore that the differences in their backgrounds had never been more glaringly obvious. While she was filled with nervousness and awe over using a priceless museum piece, Murad simply viewed it as a nice-looking carpet. But she didn't want to dwell on their differences, she told herself. She wanted to enjoy their similarities. A slight flush warmed her cheeks as she remembered the best example of how well they fit together.

Relegating her worries about their relationship to the back of her mind, she concentrated instead on Murad's problem. That was one place where he really did need her, and she had no intention of failing him.

"We could hold the party during working hours so that no one will have an excuse not to show. And could you stifle your scruples about alcohol long enough to have an open bar? It may be underhanded, but alcohol does tend to loosen tongues."

"If that's your definition of underhanded, you'll never make it as a spy." Murad chuckled. "And the alcohol is no problem. I won't serve it in my home, but the office is hardly home."

"Don't let Walton hear you say that. Your investment firm is his whole life."

"No," Murad said slowly. "The power it represents is what appeals to Walton. Being the one in charge is an obsession with him, which is why I don't think he's our thief. I don't think he'd risk his position just for money. He doesn't begin to spend what he has now. He actually lives a relatively ascetic life and has done for over twenty years. I checked him out very thoroughly."

"I still don't like him. He's a rude, nasty, vicious twerp!"

"But other than that . . ." Murad laughed.

"How can you laugh," Eleanore protested, "when he treats you like something that just crawled out from under a rock."

"Because I know I'm not," Murad said calmly. "Walton's opinion of me is irrelevant to what I am."

"And you also have the option of squashing him any time you want?" Eleanore made a shrewd guess.

"That, too." Murad's eyes twinkled.

"Well, I don't," she grumbled.

"Poor Eleanore." Murad reached across the seat and took her hand. "You're simply out of sorts."

"Of course I'm out of sorts! I've had a ghastly day."

"Poor baby," Murad sympathized.

Eleanore stared into his gleaming black eyes, watching in mesmerized fascination as their velvety depths caught the reflected sunlight, creating the illusion of tiny fires exploding.

Instinctively, her hand clenched his as a flash of desire stained her cheekbones. She licked her dry lips, blind to everything but an overwhelming desire to kiss him.

It was not a wish Murad was willing to gratify. With a muffled expletive in Arabic that was redolent with frustration, Murad glared through the plate-glass window at the chauffeur, who, although he couldn't hear them, had a clear view of the back seat in his rearview mirror. "Always we are surrounded by people."

"It does seem that way, doesn't it." Eleanore drew comfort from the longing in his voice, which he made no attempt to disguise.

"Soon," he muttered cryptically, and Eleanore wondered what he meant. That soon they wouldn't be surrounded by people? Or that soon it wouldn't matter? Or, perhaps, he meant something entirely different. All she knew for certain was that she had no intention of asking because as long as she didn't know, she could hope. And hope was something she had no intention of relinquishing.

BUT BY THE FOLLOWING DAY she felt as if hope for a better tomorrow were all she had left. Delivering Lacey to Kelly had turned out to be much harder than she'd expected. Even the sure knowledge that it was best for Lacey's long-term interests hadn't alleviated her sense of loss. She'd returned to Murad's home fighting an overwhelming desire to sit down and cry.

To her surprise, Murad arrived home ten minutes after she did.

"What's wrong?" Eleanore demanded. "You never come home for lunch."

"I thought you might need cheering up after giving Lacey to your cousin."

Eleanore tried to smile at him, encouraged by the fact that he'd not only realized how depressed she'd feel, but that he'd been willing to alter his routine to do something about it. She opened her mouth to thank him and to both their surprise promptly burst into tears.

12

"I'M SORRY," Eleanore wailed after her crying had tapered off into a series of watery hiccups. "I don't know what's wrong with me. I never cry and here I am sobbing all over you. Again."

"You've had an extremely stressful morning," Murad's warm voice held no hint of censure and Eleanore snuggled closer to him.

The faint, clean scent of soap clung to his hand, which was resting on her shoulders beneath her cheek. She breathed deeply, then pressed her face into his neck, gently biting the tanned skin above his shirt collar. She slowly ran the tip of her finger around his ear and then rubbed the palm of her hand over the rough silk of his cheek. His emerging beard tickled her palm, sending sparkling darts of sensation dancing up her arm.

The steady beat of his heart pounding against her chest was affecting the normal rhythm of her breathing, shortening it into gasps. Tipping her head back, she began to caress his jawline with her lips, pausing at his chin to lightly flick her tongue across his firm skin. An aching desire filled her at the slightly salty taste of it.

"Eleanore, no!" His hand cupped the back of her head as if to stop her, but somehow it only seemed to press her closer.

"No?" Her lips nibbled on his earlobe. Capturing it between her teeth, she caressed it with her tongue.

"Eleanore, we can't."

"You underestimate me."

"This isn't a good idea," he insisted, knowing that he had to give her feelings time for him to develop without confusing the issue with sex. Fantastic as it was between them, he wanted more from her than a willing sexual partner. He wanted her to love him as he loved her.

"Maybe not." She managed a natural tone even though she wanted to scream with frustration. What was the matter with the man? Was his sudden reticence due to something in his Middle-Eastern background? Or was it something entirely different? She had no way of knowing. The only thing that she was entirely sure of was that she had no intention of forcing a confrontation. Not when every day that she waited strengthened the bonds between them. Time was most definitely on her side.

She opted for a safer subject. "Have you thought any more about a social function at the office?"

"Yes, I called the caterers this morning and it's set up for tomorrow afternoon."

"Tomorrow?" she asked in surprise.

"Something along the lines of 'if it were done, it were best done quickly.' The problem is that I can't seem to come up with an excuse for the party."

"I don't think you need one. I mean, you've taken a lot of time and trouble to create the image of a playboy. Is anyone really going to think it's strange that you want to play during working hours? It seems to me they'll simply think you're behaving in character."

"You may be right. How about if we plan the party from, say, four to five."

"Three to five. That'll give us time to talk to everyone without being obvious."

"For all the good it's likely to do us." Murad rubbed the back of his neck in frustration.

"Is your father going to be very angry if you don't catch the thief?" She felt a chill of fear as she remembered a few of the internecine power struggles in the Middle East she'd read about.

"My father?" Murad seemed puzzled by the question. "Why should he be mad if I give it my best shot?"

"I don't know." Eleanore shrugged. "I've never met any kings before."

"You will," Murad promised, "but enough of our elusive thief. I came home to take you out to lunch."

"Thank you, kind sir. I accept." She made a mock curtsy. "Just give me a moment to put on some makeup."

"Nonsense." Murad took her arm. "You don't need to gild the lily. You look great as you are. Come on, let's go." He urged her toward the door and Eleanore went, encased in a glow of happiness at his casual tribute.

FRUSTRATED, Eleanore eyed the chattering office staff over the rim of her glass of champagne cocktail and then glanced at the clock on the wall. Four-thirty. There was only half an hour left and it very much looked as if this party was going to be yet another failure. Apparently, the thief had better sense than to allow himself to be plied with liquor.

Unlike some of the staff. She frowned at a very junior investment counselor who was sitting in the corner, staring in total absorption at the wallpaper. Making a mental note to ask Murad to have one of his men take the young man home, she dismissed him from her mind and continued her study of the room's occupants.

They had formed themselves into virtually the same small groups as they had at each of the previous social events. Instinctively, she looked around for Murad and saw him standing at one end of the temporary bar the caterers had set up. He appeared to be listening to whatever it was that Walton was saying.

The sneer on Walton's face made Eleanore furious. Taking a fortifying sip of her drink, she continued her perusal of the staff.

The young female clerks were huddled together at the other end of the bar, giggling and occasionally stealing furtive glances at Murad. All except Beth. Eleanore smiled in sympathy as she watched Beth watching Abrams, her eyes filled with love.

Eleanore's smile faded as she realized she wasn't the only one aware of the young lovers. Ms Paulson was standing in the doorway to Walton's office, watching them. Curious, Eleanore tried to read the woman's expression. There was envy there, but it was much more complicated than that. There was also a smug complacency as well as the faintest trace of pity. But why would Ms Paulson pity Beth? Beth had Abrams's love, didn't she? Eleanore glanced back at Abrams, who was accepting Beth's open adulation as if it were his due.

Eleanore frowned, remembering how Ms Paulson had made such a determined pitch to Murad to promote Abrams's talents as worthy of a place on the actual investment team. She hadn't had one word of praise for anyone else in the office, except her boss. And that had been perfunctory. So why was she promoting Abrams's career? On the surface it didn't seem to make much sense.

Deciding that a bit of probing might be in order, Eleanore carefully made her way toward Ms Paulson, trying to give the impression of someone who'd had a little too much to drink.

"Hi there." Eleanore produced a replica of Murad's vacuous smile.

"Hi, yourself." Ms Paulson plucked Eleanore's drink out of her hand and replaced it with her own.

"Mine's soda water," she said at Eleanore's questioning glance. "Never have more than one drink at office parties. You're going to have enough trouble hanging on to Prince Charming without getting publicly drunk." The sneer in Ms Paulson's voice made Eleanore angry even as she was touched at the woman's rough concern. Telling herself that neither emotion was appropriate for an apprentice spy, Eleanore tried to use her supposed state of inebriation to her advantage.

"At least, I've got a man. Which is more than can be said for you." Eleanore forced herself to give Ms Paulson a disparaging once-over. "Even a junior staffer like Beth has herself a man."

"Why you—" Ms Paulson sputtered, her face unbecomingly flushed.

Encouraged by the first break she'd ever seen in the woman's composure, Eleanore continued in a commiserating tone. "You missed a good bet there. Abrams was right under your nose and you let Beth nip in and steal him." Eleanore heaved a sympathetic sigh. "Too bad."

"She did not steal him," Ms Paulson hissed. "She's simply a blind."

"Blind?" Eleanore blinked owlishly. "No, she isn't. She sees just fine."

"She's a diversion because Walton doesn't allow his senior staff to date each other, but she's so far down the office chain of command, it doesn't matter. But once Walton's gone, then you'll see." Ms Paulson gloated. "Then Todd will get the promotion I've been priming him for and we can get married."

"Mr. Walton is leaving? Oh, goody. I don't like him." Eleanore's enthusiasm was unfeigned.

"Shh." Ms Paulson glanced around them in dismay. "I shouldn't have said that, since nothing's decided yet, but he's talking about going out on his own. So don't you say anything to His Excellency," she warned. "Not that you'll remember this when you sober up."

Now that was very interesting, Eleanore thought as she watched her walk over to the bar. Ms Paulson considered Todd Abrams committed to her. Whatever else Ms Paulson was, she wasn't stupid. If she thought Abrams was only romancing Beth as a blind, and that she and he were going to be married in the not-too-distant future, then it was because he'd told her so.

What else had she said? Eleanore mentally reviewed the conversation. That when Abrams got the promotion that she was priming him for... Could that be it? Could her priming have included information on pending land acquisitions? It made sense. Excitement began to bubble through her.

Suppose Abrams had romanced Ms Paulson in order to get the confidential information he needed? And then had asked her to keep it a secret, not because he was worried about what Walton would say about his top staff dating, but because he didn't want anyone to know that he'd had access to the information. He certainly would have the ability and the means to make full use of any information that Ms Paulson might have given him.

Eleanore glanced down at the floor to hide the triumph glowing in her face. She'd done it! She'd found the thief! She, and not Murad, with all his contacts.

At least she thought she had. A momentary doubt shook her as she glanced at Abrams. He certainly didn't look like a criminal. And she really had no hard proof. So what did she do now? Tell Murad what she suspected? No, she decided, not yet. First, she was going to have a go at surprising a damaging admission out of Abrams.

She watched as Abrams headed down the hall toward his office.

There was no time like the present, Eleanore told herself with barely contained excitement. She could almost see the expression on Murad's face when she presented him with the solution to the thefts.

Absently handing her glass to a passing waiter, Eleanore followed Abrams, being careful not to be too obvious. She found him in his office, seated at his desk.

"Why, Miss Fulton." Abrams got to his feet, his expression questioning. "Have you lost your way?"

"That should be *my* line."

"I beg your pardon?" He gave her a charming smile.

"I was referring to your little excursion into fraud."

"Fraud? What are you talking about?" Abrams's laugh sounded slightly strained to Eleanore's ears.

"I'm talking about the use you made of the inside information you got from Ms Paulson." Eleanore watched as his face suddenly went three shades paler.

He sank down into his desk chair, never taking his eyes off her. "I hardly think that the ravings of a jealous woman—"

"Oh, but she isn't jealous. The poor fool honestly believes you're going to marry her just as soon as you get your promotion."

"There's no fool like an old fool," Abrams said flippantly.

Angry at his callous dismissal of his unwitting partner, Eleanore snapped, "She'll have the last laugh, though. Just as soon as I tell Murad . . ."

Her voice trailed off as Abrams slowly raised his hand, which had been out of sight behind the desk. Eleanore blinked in disbelief as she found herself staring down the muzzle of a deadly-looking handgun. Somehow, it had never occurred to her that she might be in any physical danger. There hadn't even been a hint of violence attached to the case. Until now. She studied Abrams. If his trembling was any indication, he was extremely nervous. The knowledge helped to still her rising sense of panic. If she just kept her head, she might be able to outwit him.

"So I was right." Abrams slowly got to his feet, and, keeping the gun pointed at her, carefully closed his office door. "There is more to Ahiqar than just a playboy. How much more?" he demanded.

Uncertain of how much to tell him and how much to hold back, Eleanore opted for part of the truth. "His father asked him to find out who's been stealing from the company."

"That old bastard!" Abrams bit out. "Do you know what he's worth? Billions! And he's after the few million I made."

"The few million you stole!" Anger overcame her discretion.

"Shut up while I think." He waved the gun at her and Eleanore subsided, afraid he'd accidentally shoot her. He didn't handle the weapon as if he were familiar with it.

"I have to get out of here." He opened the door a crack and peeked out. The sound of the party drifted down the hallway.

Abrams rubbed his hand over the sheen of sweat on his forehead. "Now you listen real good, lady." He gestured with the gun for emphasis. "We're going to leave. I'm going to put my gun in my suit-jacket pocket and you're to stick to me like glue while we go out the back way."

"And where are we going?" Eleanore stalled for time.

"My apartment. So I can think." His voice shook. "Get over here." He grabbed her by the arm and jerked her up against him.

Eleanore winced as the muzzle of the gun bit into her side.

"If you try to attract any attention as we leave . . ."

"I know. You'll shoot me," she said, trying to decide if it would be smarter to risk a confrontation now or later.

"Oh, no, lady. You're my ticket out of here. I'll shoot whoever tries to come to your rescue."

Eleanore's stomach lurched as an image of Murad's bleeding body filled her mind. Abrams just might carry out his threat. He was certainly frightened enough.

Deciding that her best bet would be to go along with him until she could come up with a plan of action, she said, "Don't worry. I won't give you any trouble."

True to her word, she offered no resistance as he forced her out through the back of the building and into a cab.

Twenty minutes later, the bored cabbie deposited them in front of Abrams's apartment building without ever having suspected that there was anything unusual about his fare.

"Remember what I told you," Abrams hissed as he steered her across the lobby, "and you won't get hurt."

"I'll remember." She kept her voice steady with an effort.

"See that you do." He motioned her into the empty elevator and pushed the button for the fourth floor.

Abrams unlocked his apartment door and shoved her inside. "Sit down." He pulled the gun out of his pocket and gestured toward the couch. "I've got to think."

Eleanore obediently subsided onto the couch, grateful that he seemed a little calmer now that they were on his home turf.

Abrams sank down onto one of the armchairs across from her and appeared to be deep in thought.

Surreptitiously, Eleanore glanced around, looking for something she could use as a weapon. Abrams might claim he didn't want to hurt her, but she didn't place a great deal of hope on his adhering to that viewpoint if it came to a choice between her life or his freedom. Unfortunately, the ceramic coffee table in front of her was totally bare, as were the two end tables on either side of the couch. There were no ornaments or objets d'art or even ashtrays that, in a pinch, she could use to defend herself.

She looked down at her hands as if assessing them as weapons and was vaguely surprised to find they were shaking. She closed her eyes against the revealing sight and took a deep, steadying breath, trying to dispel the faint sense of nausea twisting through her. She had to keep calm. Her only chance of escaping depended on being alert enough to take advantage of any opportunity that presented itself.

"I've got it," Abrams exclaimed.

"Got what?" Eleanore asked, feeling that if she could just keep him talking she'd be safe.

"How to keep you quiet while I leave the country tonight."

"You want to leave? Leave. I'm not going to try to stop you." She tried a smile that wavered ever so slightly around the edges.

"Lady, I wouldn't trust you any farther than I could throw you. No, when I leave I want you well out of it."

"Oh?" Eleanore stared in horrified fascination at his gun, trying to work up the courage to attack him.

"You're going to take two—no, better make that four—sleeping pills. That should keep you unconscious until tomorrow when I'll be safely in Brazil."

"Brazil? Why would you want to go to Brazil?" she asked, wondering why he'd tell her his destination if he didn't intend to kill her.

"Brazil doesn't have an extradition treaty with America," he said shortly, pointing across the room with his gun. "The bathroom's that way. The sooner you swallow those pills, the sooner I can get to the airport."

Reluctantly Eleanore rose, not wanting to take that many sleeping pills, but more afraid that if she refused he might opt for a more permanent method of getting her out of the way.

"Hurry up," he snapped. "I haven't got all—"

The sudden chime of the doorbell echoed through the apartment with the impact of an explosion.

"What the hell?" Abrams stared nervously at the door. "Someone must have seen me come in." He shifted uncertainly as the doorbell rang again.

"Get over against the wall behind the door." He waited until she'd complied and then he secreted the gun behind his back. "If you so much as open your mouth . . ." His tense features sharpened Eleanore's feeling of impending disaster.

"I won't," she assured him.

"Who's there?" Abrams shouted through the door.

"It's just me, Mr. Abrams. Willis, the janitor. I got an Express that was delivered to you this afternoon. The office told me to bring it up."

"An Express?" Abrams relaxed slightly.

"Yeah. A bulky envelope from someplace in Switzerland, I think it says."

"Switzerland?" Abrams repeated and then, making up his mind, used his free hand to unlock the door and swing it open.

The janitor suddenly yelped and scuttled sideways, giving Abrams the instant warning he needed.

"Freeze, you bastard." He pointed the gun at someone in the hall. "I've got a gun."

"He does," Eleanore yelled, trying to warn whoever was there.

"That, I don't doubt for a minute." The sound of Murad's deep voice filled Eleanore with despair. It was bad enough that she was in this fix, but at least Abrams bore her no personal ill will. Murad he quite obviously hated.

"Get in here and shut the door." Abrams retreated as Murad slowly entered the apartment.

"Are you all right, Eleanore?" Murad shot her a quick, assessing glance.

"Yeah. I found your thief." She gestured toward the visibly trembling Abrams. "And I've got another news flash for you. I'm turning in my Junior G-man badge," she quipped, trying to lighten the smoldering atmosphere.

Murad's lips lifted in a reluctant smile. "Just as well. The first requirement of a spy is forethought."

"Would you two shut up?" Abrams's voice cracked. "That damned janitor has probably run right to the police!"

"No. My men will intercept him. I don't want any witnesses." Murad's chill voice sent a wave of apprehension through Eleanore. He sounded absolutely pitiless. She glanced at Abrams. Apparently, he shared her assessment of Murad's state of mind for his trembling increased.

"The pills won't work," Abrams muttered to himself, "because of your men. Even if you're unconscious, they won't let me leave." He gnawed on his lower lip. "I need some way to get past them. Get over here," he suddenly ordered Eleanore.

Slowly, Eleanore complied until she was within his grasp. He grabbed her arm and jerked her up against his left side, his gun still aimed at Murad's chest.

"She's my ticket out of here. You won't dare to make a move against me while I've got her." A satisfied smirk lit Abrams's face. "Because you know I'd kill her, don't you?"

"I'd make a better hostage," Murad's clipped voice gave Eleanore a clue to the anger gripping him.

"Oh, no." Abrams shook his head. "Who know what tricks you might pull? Whereas your friend here—" he nodded toward Eleanore "—she's too smart to try anything. Aren't you, honey?"

Eleanore studied Murad's hard, determined features in despair. His black eyes seemed to glow with incandescent flames. Somehow, she knew he wasn't going to let her leave the apartment with Abrams. He'd try to stop them and probably get himself shot in the process. Grimly, she fought back the raw panic that filled her at the thought of a world without Murad in it. She slowly expelled her breath, trying to think. She had to help Murad by providing a distraction. Even if it were only for a second, it might be enough to give him an edge. She remembered his lightning-quick reflexes the night she'd been mugged.

Not giving herself time to think about it, she gave a realistic groan and said, "I'm going to throw up." Her fear for Murad's safety gave her words added authenticity.

"What the—" Abrams swung his head toward her and Murad sprang at him. Abrams didn't have a chance. Five seconds later he was sprawled unconscious on the floor.

"You idiot, you could have gotten yourself killed," Eleanore yelled at Murad, her relief giving way to anger.

"*I'm* an idiot!" he yelled back. "Who was the numbskull who confronted him?"

"I confronted an embezzler. How was I supposed to know he'd turn into Billy the Kid right before my eyes?"

"Common sense?" Murad pulled her into his arms. "Experience?"

"I haven't got any experience." She snuggled against him, wincing as she felt his chest shake with laughter. "As a spy," she added. "Besides, I was so elated that I'd managed to solve the crime that I wanted to wrap up the loose ends."

"And, instead, almost got wrapped up yourself. When I realized that he'd abducted you..." Murad shuddered.

Eleanore studied the white lines around his mouth, feeling elated at the visible sign of his concern for her.

"How did you figure out what had happened so quickly?" she asked curiously. "You were right behind me."

"From now on I intend to be one step ahead of you," Murad vowed. "I'd been watching you all afternoon."

"You had?" She blinked in surprise.

"You were the most watchable thing there. When I saw you go down the hallway, I thought you were going to the rest room. But when you didn't come back, I went looking for you. I found your purse in Abrams's office, where you'd dropped it. A call down to the guard in the lobby confirmed that you had left with him. So I checked his address in the personnel files and raced over here, hoping he'd want to pick up some stuff before bolting."

"He didn't want to hurt me." Eleanore glanced down at Abrams, who was still sprawled on the floor. "The situation simply blew up in his face and he didn't know what to do. You didn't really hurt him, did you?"

"No, but he's going to have a splitting headache when he wakes up."

"I wish you'd teach me how to do that," she said wistfully. "Your instructor was better than mine."

"You won't need the knowledge. Your career as a fledgling spy has come to an abrupt end. My nerves can't take any more of this."

His arms tightened and he lowered his head, his lips meeting hers with a driving hunger he made no attempt to hide. His fingers speared through her hair and his mouth forced her lips apart. Eleanore shivered as his tongue ran over the velvety inside of her cheek.

Instinctively, she pressed closer, her breasts pushing into the hard wall of his chest. Her fingertips slowly caressed his cheek and the raspy, silken feel of his freshly shaven skin darted along her nerve endings.

A soft, yearning sound of pure desire bubbled out of her throat to be swallowed by his demanding mouth. A demand Eleanore reveled in, seeing it as proof of his need for her. Her feeling of euphoria was abruptly shattered at the sound of splintering wood.

Suddenly, she found herself standing alone, while Murad barked out a command in Arabic.

Blinking to clear her passion-fogged mind, she stared down at Abrams. He was now stirring, the more humanitarian part of her mind was pleased to note, but he hadn't made the noise. Confused, she turned around and found herself staring at six men carrying an arsenal of weapons that would have given an army battalion pause.

"You are all right, Excellency?" It was the man Eleanore recognized as having been with Murad the night she'd been mugged.

"As you can see. There's our thief." Murad nodded toward the now groaning Abrams.

"Take him down to the police station," Murad ordered. "I'll be down later to press charges."

Eleanore moved back as they collected Abrams and half carried, half dragged him out of the apartment.

A hot flash of intense anger effectively doused her desire. Even after what they'd just been through he still didn't want his household to see that he regarded her as more than a friend of the family. She did something she rarely did and thoroughly lost her temper.

"Now, where were we?" Murad gave her a slow, seductive smile and reached for her.

"I don't know about you, but I was leaving," Eleanore snapped. "Leaving this benighted apartment, your damned house, this—"

"What's wrong?" Murad peered worriedly at her. "A second ago you were melting in my arms—"

"Only until there were witnesses," she yelled at him. "I'm sick to death of the way you're always so very careful not to let any of your household see you in a compromising position! I'll help you deal with your narrow-minded compatriots. I'll leave."

"Like hell you will!" Murad bit out. "I was trying to give your feelings for me time to develop without using sex to push you into anything. I knew we'd made love too soon. That you were emotionally off balance from that meeting with your father that I'd forced on you. But once I'd kissed you..." He grimaced. "I couldn't stop myself."

Eleanore studied him uncertainly, trying to decipher his exact meaning. Could he possibly mean he loved her? Just a little? There was only one way to find out. Taking a deep breath, she decided to gamble.

"I made love to you because I'm in love with you," she blurted out and then stared down at the honey-beige carpet, afraid to look at him for fear of the reaction she might read on his face.

To her amazement, she found herself grabbed and swung in an exuberant circle.

"Murad!" She clutched his shoulders. "What's the matter with you?"

"What's the matter with me?" he repeated incredulously. "You just handed me the answer to my fervent prayers and you ask me why I'm excited."

"Prayers?" Eleanore stared into his glowing face and the hard knot of uncertainty in her chest slowly began to dissolve.

"I love you, Eleanore Fulton. Totally, passionately, extravagantly." He swung her around again.

"Really? You aren't just saying that because we caught the thief?" She was almost afraid to believe him.

"No, because you are intelligent, loyal, beautiful and sexy. Especially sexy. And speaking of sexy—come on, let's go." He set her back on her feet and, taking her hand, began to pull her toward the door.

"Go where?" She hurried along beside him.

"To the airport. To grab the first plane we can find to Las Vegas to get married. They don't have a waiting period."

"You want to marry me?" she gasped.

"Eleanore, haven't you been listening to anything I said? Why do you think I went to so much trouble to protect your reputation? Because I was hoping you'd be spending the rest of your life around my narrow-minded staff."

"The rest of my life?" Eleanore repeated his words and found them intoxicating.

"You will marry me, won't you? I mean a real marriage. I don't want to stifle you. You can keep your teaching job. I can rearrange my schedule to do quite a bit of my work at home once we have a baby."

"A baby?" Eleanore felt her cup of happiness run over. At long last she was going to have a family of her own.

"I really appreciate your offer, Murad, but I don't think I'll go back to my old job. Since I won't have to worry about earning a living, I'd like to volunteer my expertise to the adult literacy program at the Y. They have such a need."

"Speaking of need . . ." Murad's husky voice sent her heart rate skyrocketing. She loved him so much. Unexpectedly, an image of Beth flashed through her mind and she winced.

"What's wrong, darling?"

"I was just thinking of Beth and poor Ms Paulson. They're not only going to be heartbroken, but the whole office will know about it. Can't you do something?"

"I suppose I could transfer them to other offices. Maybe Beth to London and Ms Paulson to Paris? Coping with new countries should keep them busy."

"Thanks." Eleanore beamed at him.

"For you, love, I'd do anything." He dropped a quick kiss on the tip of her nose. "Now, enough of other people's problems. You promised to marry me."

"Try to stop me. Come on." She urged him toward the elevator at the end of the hall. "The sooner we apply for a license, the sooner we can get married and make love whenever and wherever we want." She flushed slightly, but met his loving gaze squarely.

"I've got a better idea," Murad said. "We'll charter a jet and make love all the way to Las Vegas."

"Now that's what I like." Eleanore laughed, feeling light-headed with happiness. "A man with imagination."

"Darling, you haven't seen anything yet."

HARLEQUIN Temptation

COMING NEXT MONTH

Your favorite stories with a brand-new look!!

HARLEQUIN
American Romance®

Beginning next month, the four American Romance titles will feature a new, contemporary and sophisticated cover design. As always, each story will be a terrific romance with mature characters and a realistic plot that is uniquely North American in flavor and appeal.

Watch your bookshelves for a **bold** look!

ARNC-1

Harlequin American Romance

Romances that go one step farther...
American Romance

Realistic stories involving people you can relate to and
care about.

Compelling relationships between the mature men and
women of today's world.

Romances that capture the core of genuine emotions
between a man and a woman.

Join us each month for four new titles wherever paperback
books are sold.
Enter the world of American Romance.

Amro-1

Coming in June...

PENNY JORDAN

a reason for being

We invite you to join us in celebrating Harlequin's 40th Anniversary with this very special book we selected to publish worldwide.

While you read this story, millions of women in 100 countries will be reading it, too.

A Reason for Being by Penny Jordan is being published in June in the Presents series in 19 languages around the world. Join women around the world in helping us to celebrate 40 years of romance.

Penny Jordan's *A Reason for Being* is Presents June title #1180. Look for it wherever paperbacks are sold.